"Carla and Peter Weber move to a small town in California's Sierra foothills. Peter runs into problems with his job as a bank president and their marriage is in trouble. Carla reacts by falling in love with another woman's house, a ruined antebellum-style mansion. She knows she's being irrational, but she can't help feeling that if she and Peter could only live in the house they would regain their lost happiness. Carla wangles a job helping to restore the building and when the owner is murdered, she uses her new-found knowledge of local history to track down the killer."

Sierra Gothic
by
Merrill Sanders

Credits
Cover Drawing: Janette K. Hopper
Front: "Foggy Morning"
Back: "Foggy Morning," (flipped horizontally)
http//janettekhopper.com

ISBN 1-931333-22-X

LCCN 2002115125

Dry Bones Press
POB 597
Roseville, CA 95678
http://www.drybones.com
drybones@drybones.com

First Edition
Fiction

Sierra Gothic

by

Merrill Sanders

Dry Bones Press
Rocklin, California

Chapter 1

Carla didn't want to go to the afternoon tea party. Her hostess, Josie Kettering, was a bad joke, and she had a good idea that she wouldn't like any of the other guests, either. "Rats," she muttered as she gave her long brown hair a final vicious swipe with the hairbrush. She straightened her skirt, shouldered her purse and set off on foot for the high-rent section of town.

She'd met Josie the day before and they'd tangled like an elderly tomcat and a new kitten the owner has just introduced into the house. As usual, Carla had forgotten to go to the grocery store. She'd been waiting her turn in line at the village delicatessen to buy last-minute sandwiches for dinner when Josie tapped her on the shoulder.

Josie was in her sixties, an imposing presence. Her short gray hair was set in curls that could only have come fresh from the beauty shop and her barrel-shaped body was encased in a cool looking white linen dress. Carla was wearing her jeans and a ratty sweatshirt and the older woman gave her the uncomfortable feeling that she should have changed before she left home.

"You're Carla Weber, aren't you?" Josie had an unpleasantly loud voice.

Carla nodded.

"I'm Josie Kettering. My husband is Howard Kettering, President of the First National Bank of Placer Bar. I believe somebody pointed you out to me at the Memorial Day parade. Your husband is the manager of the new Cal-Equity Savings office, isn't he?"

"That's right."

"It's nice to have a savings and loan branch in our little community, although I can't get used to the idea of a financial institution operating out of a trailer. It seems so—so fly-by-night." Josie's voice had grown even louder and she was drawling her words. She seemed to assume that everyone in the store was interested in what she had to say.

"They plan to replace the trailer with a regular building later this year," Carla said stiffly, broadcasting a little herself. She was standing face-to-face with the other woman so they weren't actually shouting, but they were making enough noise for people to turn and look at them. "Most of Cal-Equity's branches start out in trailers. This one is nothing special."

"I wouldn't know about that." Josie preened. "The First National has been in its present location since before the turn of the century. It was started by my husband's grandfather, Davis Kettering. You might say the Ketterings built this town."

"I'll have two pastramis on rye, with everything, to go," Carla told the man behind the counter. She'd reached the head of the service line.

"I'm picking up a few last minute things for a party I'm giving tomorrow," Josie continued as the man assembled Carla's sandwiches. "Some ladies are coming by in the afternoon for tea. Would you care to join us? It's so important to meet the right people when you move to a new town."

It was obvious that Josie was only inviting her because of Peter's job. Carla was about to refuse when she thought about her husband and the quarrel they'd just had.

She'd spent the day fishing again and, as usual, the time

had slipped away from her. Peter's car had been in the driveway when she got home. Hoping to avoid trouble, she'd slipped through the side yard and in by the back door, her full creel bumping guiltily against her wet leg.

Peter had flown into a rage when he caught her sneaking into the house like a teenager after a late date. "You can't go on hiding from the world like this, wandering the streams with your fishing pole" he'd yelled. "Why can't you make a few friends? At the very least, you could interrupt your fishing for long enough to get to the grocery store. I'd give anything to have a normal meal for a change."

Her fishing really bothered Peter. He said it was escapist, that she was withdrawing from life in general and him in particular, and she couldn't tell him he was wrong. But Peter was impossible to get along with these days, and this town had turned out to be sheer poison for their marriage. Fishing filled the long, lonely hours.

Carla looked at Josie's expectant face and thought quickly. If she agreed to go to the party, Peter might stop giving her such a hard time—and if he didn't, at least it would be something she could use in her own defense the next time they had a fight. "Okay," she muttered ungraciously. "What time do you want me to be there?"

"Around two o'clock. It's the big house at the corner of Oak and Broad Streets. You can't miss it."

* * *

Now she was regretting the impulse that had led her to accept the invitation. Placer Bar was a pretty place, she admitted as she walked through the Historical District, but the town and its inhabitants had nothing to offer her. The commercial center was a tangle of narrow streets lined with tin-roofed wooden commercial buildings, most of them only one or two stories high, with Western false fronts to make them look more imposing. Bright street banners advertising Pioneer Days, the town's annual festival, flapped cheerfully in the sun. A range of green-gray mountains made a striking background.

An old mining community in California's Sierra foothills, Placer Bar attracted hoards of sightseers in the spring and summer, hunters in the fall, and skiers in the winter. Like most communities that depend on tourism, Placer Bar was divided strictly into locals and outsiders. Carla was an outsider and would always be one. They'd only been here three months, but she knew she'd never fit in.

The Kettering house was far up Broad Street in the old residential section, an imposing gray stone structure on a corner lot. No wonder Josie had sneered at the idea of a bank in a trailer, Carla thought as she pushed the bell. If something went wrong at the First National, they could move the bank into their house and defend it from an army of bank robbers. The place was built like a fort.

The door was opened by one of the local teenagers, a girl with short purple hair, part of a group that Carla had seen at the shopping mall at the edge of town. Today she was wearing a severe black-and-white uniform that looked like it dated from the 1940's and she'd even pinned a white lace handkerchief on top of her head. She welcomed Carla with a hundred-watt smile. The girl was obviously having a wonderful time playing a maid in an old-fashioned drawing room comedy.

She showed Carla into a large, pleasant living room. Tall French windows at the back of the house let in a generous amount of light. The furniture was expensive looking but not particularly appealing. Overstuffed sofas and chairs upholstered in beige linen were arranged in a formal group on an Oriental rug near the hall, and a second, more casual, arrangement of dark blue chairs occupied the space near the windows leading out into the garden.

Josie's ample figure was clad in a fussy silk skirt and blouse costume. She sat primly in the exact center of a love seat in the formal beige group of furniture, her hands folded in her lap. In front of her was a glass-topped coffee table with a tea service in its center, a two-pot antique silver job. The tea tray was flanked by plates of small sandwiches; roast beef with cucumber, ham with pickle and smoked salmon with cream cheese. There were bowls holding celery and olives and even the side tables were covered with small silver dishes of nuts and bonbons. Josie was staring at the food anxiously, a small frown on her face, as if she expected a bug to crawl out from under one of the sandwiches and was determined to deal firmly with the insect when this happened.

She looked up as Carla entered the room. "You're right on time." Without waiting for a response, she waved Carla to the sofa, then turned to an ancient woman sitting in a wing chair that partly hid her face. "I'd like you to meet Maud Rucker. Maud's from an old Placer Bar family. Her people have lived here since the Gold Rush days. Maud, this is Carla Weber. Her husband runs the new Cal-Equity Savings office."

Maud leaned forward to acknowledge the introduction. Her frail figure was draped in a flower-print cotton dress that had seen too many washings, and her hair was thin and shapelessly arranged, gathered at the nape of her neck in a wispy bun. Her eyes shone appraisingly from a nest of wrinkles as Carla shook her hand.

Two other guests came into the room as Carla murmured a greeting. She recognized the woman on the left, Sally Bolt, a widow. Her husband had owned a logging firm, but she'd sold it when he died. Sally was in her early forties, about ten years older than Carla, and they'd met at a Chamber of Commerce party. Sally had spent the evening flirting with the men on the dance floor and Carla had been struck by her air of frantic gaiety. Today she seemed reserved, almost depressed, although she was wearing purple eyeshadow and her mane of long black hair was tied back with a cheerful crimson ribbon.

Josie introduced the other woman as Pat Graedon. Carla hadn't met Pat before, but she'd heard of the Graedons from Peter. Pat and her husband, Lucas, owned the Miner's Palace Hotel, a fifteen room bed-and-breakfast establishment that boasted the only really good restaurant in the county. The Graedons had restored their Gold Rush brick building and furnished it with antiques.

Sally sat next to Carla on the sofa and Pat took an armchair. Pat was an unusually tall, thin woman in a well-cut gingham dress that gave her a self-consciously countrified look. One hand played restlessly with the beads at her neckline as she sat forward on the edge of her seat. She seemed ill at ease, although there was no apparent reason for this. Carla guessed she was just the nervous type.

Josie obviously felt her party had been launched. "Just how long have you lived in Placer Bar?" she asked Carla. She handed her a plate of small sandwiches and started to pour the tea, filling a delicate cup with strong liquid from the first silver teapot and diluting it with steaming hot water from the second.

"We moved here in April, just in time for Cal-Equity's Grand Opening."

"Yes, I remember—all those balloons. It was quite a circus. It seemed like every child in town was holding a balloon with your company's name on it." Josie's voice grew louder. "I was surprised to see a savings and loan opening a new office, though. I've heard most of them are losing money these days."

Carla was taken aback. Had Josie invited her here to grill her on the state of her husband's business? "The branch is doing

10

very well," she lied, taking a sandwich and passing the plate to Sally.

"I'm glad to hear it. Howard, my husband, has been worried about you."

Carla could tell by the way Josie was looking at her that the older woman hadn't believed her disclaimer. She fixed her hostess with a steely stare. "It is normal for financial institutions to experience disintermediation in periods of economic recession, but Cal-Equity's spread is reasonably close to the industry average," she intoned. What Carla was saying was that people were withdrawing money at a tremendous rate, and Peter's company was doing worse than most at a time when all savings and loans were in trouble, but she knew her words would give the opposite impression.

Peter had warned her not to talk about his business problems. "If people knew how much money we've been losing there'd be a run on the bank. If anybody asks questions, just spout some jargon. They won't understand what you're saying and they'll change the subject."

The strategy worked. Josie gave Carla a baffled look and turned to Pat Graedon. "I went by the hotel the other day. Your roses are lovely, especially the yellow ones against the east wall. Of course, the blossoms aren't as well formed as the ones in my garden. You must remind me to show you my roses before you leave. The bushes are a mass of color."

"Your roses are a different variety. Of course they look different." Pat took a chocolate from the dish at her side. She bit into it, then peered absently at the creamy filling.

"If you like, I'll give you a few cuttings. You could try grafting them onto your plants." Josie's voice was heavy with concern. She was behaving as though Pat's inferior roses were a serious problem.

Carla suppressed a giggle. She was beginning to take

Josie's measure. Josie didn't mean to be offensive; she just had a compulsion to be the first in everything. She needed to prove that her husband's bank was more successful than Peter's and that her roses were superior to the ones at the hotel. If somebody sneezed, no doubt she would claim that she had a bigger and better head cold.

As Pat and Josie went on bickering about their gardens, Carla glanced around the room.

Maud Rucker was taking full advantage of the food. She'd been eating steadily since the plates started on their rounds and she showed no sign of stopping.

Sally wasn't paying attention to the conversation either. She was staring at the fingernails of her left hand with a preoccupied air. Her mouth drooped at the edges and she seemed older and more careworn than she had on the night of the Chamber of Commerce dance.

Carla turned back to their hostess. Josie was describing her composting methods. "I find that eggshells are a great help and I mix in coffee grounds, but not too many of them." She lowered her voice and leaned toward Pat. "I'll tell you my real secret. I water my roses with a solution containing fish emulsion."

"Plain old commercial rose food works fine for me."

"That's why my roses always take first prize at the County Fair!" Josie had triumphed again. "There's another technique I'd like to try. I've heard the thing to do is bury whole fish near your rose bushes. The nutrients leach into the soil and it's a perfect organic fertilizer."

"I learned about that in third grade," Pat said. "The Indians taught that trick to the Pilgrims. They used it to grow corn, though."

Carla thought she saw a twinkle in Pat's eye. Was she leading Josie on?

If so, Josie didn't seem to notice. "I'd try it, only I have such a large garden and fish is so expensive these days. I'd spend more on feeding the roses than I do buying food for the house. My husband would be furious."

The word "fish" finally registered. "You need fish?" Carla interrupted. "I can give you all you want. I have a freezer full of trout at home."

Josie looked at her in surprise. "I do a lot of fishing," Carla explained lamely. "My husband has gotten tired of eating my catch. You'd be doing me a favor if you took a few trout off my hands."

"That's very kind," Josie said, sounding uncertain. She didn't seem to know what to make of the offer.

"You can have some, too," Carla said, turning to Pat.

"No, thank you anyway. I'm in the hotel business and the Health Department might get after me if I started burying food scraps in the garden." This time there was no mistaking it; there was a humorous quirk to Pat's mouth. She was enjoying her little dig at Josie.

Their hostess draw herself up, offended. "I'll take a few trout if you can spare them," Sally offered, trying to make peace. "I'm no gardener, but I love to eat."

Before Carla could reply, an elegant woman came into the room. She was tall and very beautiful in a daunting sort of way. Her fair hair was smoothed back in a severe style and she was wearing a tailored suit of navy blue raw silk. Sophistication incarnate, she was definitely a standout in this small mountain town. Even the purple-haired teenager was impressed. She lingered in the doorway to gawk at her, taking in the details of her dress with eager eyes, until Josie dismissed her with a sharp nod.

"I'd like you to meet another newcomer." Josie hadn't stood up to greet the rest of them, but this time she automatically rose to her feet. "This is Bronwin Stauffer. Her husband,

Owen, is President of Stauffer Electronics, the big Sacramento computer firm. The Stauffers have rented a house here for the summer."

Bronwin smiled and walked across the room with enviable poise to join their group. She sat down on the love seat next to Josie.

A flicker of motion across the table caught Carla's eye. Maud Rucker was taking advantage of the fuss to wrap a handful of sandwiches in a paper napkin. She slipped the packet into her old-fashioned cloth purse and glanced up. Noticing that Carla was watching, she gave her a cheerful wink.

Maud had evidently reached the age where people stop caring what others think of them. Carla's grandmother had gotten like that. She'd picked up the habit of saying the most startling things simply because they were true, or because saying them happened to amuse her. Carla was in her early thirties, young enough to be embarrassed. She felt as if she'd been caught eavesdropping. She looked away quickly and found herself facing Bronwin Stauffer.

"So how do you like it here in the mountains?" She blurted out the first inane remark that came to mind.

Bronwin inclined her head graciously. "We've really taken to the place. It's a lot cooler than the Central Valley. Prettier, too. In fact, we've decided to move here permanently."

"But—what are you saying? You can't be serious!" Josie stared at Bronwin, her mouth half open in alarm. Carla could guess what was worrying her. Bronwin would make a formidable social competitor in the small world of Placer Bar.

"That'll mean a long commute for Owen," Sally said, emerging from her preoccupied mood. "Especially in winter. It takes over an hour to get to Sacramento when there's ice on the road."

"We're thinking of moving the plant here, too. The compa-

14

ny's outgrown its present building and since we have to put up a new one, we might as well do it in Placer Bar. Wages are lower here and there's not so much trouble with the unions. As you say, it's difficult for people to commute to Sacramento, and that means we'd have a captive labor force."

This was important news. Carla gave Bronwin her full attention. A new factory would mean more business for Peter's savings and loan branch—he might even start earning a profit.

"You can't build a factory here" Pat Graedon slammed her teacup down in its saucer.

"Why not?" Bronwin frowned, surprised by her vehemence.

"Can't you see? You'd ruin the character of the town." Pat's voice rose as she looked around the circle for support. "Placer Bar isn't a modern city with factories and office buildings. It's a small place that has managed to keep the spirit of the Forty-Niner days."

Bronwin shrugged off this objection. "You need more industry in the area. Half the people who live here are unemployed loggers."

Sally flushed, and Carla remembered that her husband had owned a logging company. Bronwin wasn't scoring any points for tact. Still, Carla had to agree. The town desperately needed jobs.

Pat wasn't through talking. "You have to understand—a major electronics plant would bring in new people. They'd be followed by fast food restaurants and chain stores. Before you know it, there'd be housing developments and used car lots all over the place. The gold town atmosphere would be destroyed, and the tourists would stop coming here!"

Pat was worried about her hotel, of course, but she seemed sincere in her desire to protect the town from mushrooming commercial development. It was the old dilemma, jobs versus

15

preservation. Carla leaned on the side of jobs—she had to, because of Peter's work—but she had a lot of sympathy for Pat's point of view. Small, authentic and special was what Placer Bar had going for it.

Bronwin's mouth twitched in irritation. "Owen isn't going to put his plant in the middle of the Historical District. Your old-timey buildings and cute shops will be safe."

"That's not the point. I don't care if you build a wall around it, a factory would change the whole character of the town." Pat pulled herself up. "I'm going to call a meeting of the Historical Society and organize a petition to keep big industry out of Placer Bar."

Josie made an approving "harrumphing" noise. It was clear that she was on Pat's side.

"I don't think you'll get very far with your petition," Bronwin. "My husband's company has a real future. If we bring the factory here, it'll be the biggest thing to hit this town since the Gold Rush."

Maud swallowed a mouthful of food. "A factory sounds like a good idea to me," she said.

It was the first time she'd spoken and they all turned to look at her.

"The trouble with Placer Bar is, there's nothing to keep the young people here. They grow up and they can't find work, so they move away. A factory would encourage them to stay home where they belong."

Nobody had a reply to this. They were all too busy with their own thoughts to worry about the town's unemployed youth.

"Are you planning to buy a house?" Sally was still interested in the Stauffers' domestic arrangements.

"We've found a place already—the old Kettering mansion. The big house with the pillars on the outskirts of town."

"You can't be talking about Davis Kettering's house." Josie's voice was sharp. "Why, that old place has fallen into ruins. Nobody's lived there for over twenty years! Hasn't it been condemned by the city?"

"We'll have to restore it, of course." Bronwin was serene. "I want to make it look the way it did when it was first built. We'll put in a modern kitchen and baths, but the rest of the house will be historically correct. I'm looking forward to it. It should be a lot of fun."

Josie looked at Bronwin for a long moment, then leaned to one side and spoke in a stage whisper to Pat Graedon. "The Stauffers obviously don't have any family background. She thinks she can just go out and buy herself a place in the world."

Carla could hear Josie from clear across the coffee table. Bronwin, who was sitting next to her, certainly caught the insult.

Josie raised her voice and addressed Bronwin directly. "Old houses are miserable to live in. Those high ceilings—you can't keep them warm in winter. And I'm sure Davis's house is in terrible shape, with dry rot and crumbling plaster. I hear it's overrun with rats, too."

Bronwin smiled and a hard light shone in her eyes. "You can't discourage me. The house will be a showplace by the time I'm through with it. It's a beautiful building and it should have been restored a long time ago."

She rose to her feet. "I must be going. It's been an interesting afternoon."

Chapter 2

Bronwin's departure broke up the party. Josie Kettering and Pat Graedon withdrew to the far end of the living room where they stood talking in low tones, laying plans to deal with the Stauffer invasion. "Who does she think she is?" Carla heard Josie wail at one point. The heavy-set matron sounded like a young girl who'd been treated unfairly for the first time in her life, more outraged than seriously worried.

Pat was a fighter and she didn't have any doubts that they were in trouble. "The Stauffers have a lot of money," she said. "We'll have to work fast if we intend to stop the factory."

Carla considered joining their council of war, just for the fun of it, but then she rejected the idea. She didn't care what the Stauffers did so long as it didn't hurt Peter's business—and if they brought a lot of new jobs to town, it was sure to help.

Sally Bolt caught her eye. "I suppose we might as well leave," she said quietly.

Maud deposited her plate on the coffee table. "I'm going to look for that young girl who showed us in. She wandered off with my sweater and goodness knows what she's done with it." Without waiting for a reply, she disappeared through the archway into the hall, hobbling on one stiff leg.

Josie glanced over as the old lady left the room and her eyes fell on Maud's cloth purse, which she'd left lying on her

18

chair. Pulling away from Pat Graedon, she put a finger to her lips in a gesture of warning. She grinned at Carla and Sally, then tiptoed with exaggerated caution through a doorway in a side wall. She must have visited the kitchen for when she returned she was carrying a chunk of what looked like raw beef liver in a plastic bag. She wrapped the bag in napkins and tucked it into Maud's purse, taking the sandwiches out and dropping them into an empty coal scuttle near the fireplace. Carla was astonished by the childish trick. She didn't know what to make of such behavior.

Maud came back, struggling into a rusty black sweater, and Josie saw her to the door. She burst out laughing as she returned to the living room.

"It's been a long time since I've played a trick on old Maud—it makes me feel like a kid again. We used to have fun with her on Halloween. One year we moved her family's outhouse to the middle of Broad Street, right downtown. They had to use a chamberpot for two days until some men came and put it back on its foundation." She giggled again at the memory.

"I have to go now," Carla said, repulsed. "It's getting late." The tea party hadn't been as dull as she'd expected, but it certainly hadn't been a pleasant social experience, and this stunt of Josie's was the last straw.

Sally said her goodbyes too, and they went out the door together. Their paths lay in the same direction and Sally fell into step beside her as they set off down Broad Street.

"What did you think about that business with the raw liver?" Carla asked. The incident rankled in her mind.

"It was just a joke." Sally shrugged.

"It seemed like an awfully mean one. Judging from her clothes, Maud took those sandwiches because she needs the food."

"She can cook the liver for dinner. She probably will. From what I gather, she lives almost entirely on Social Security."

Sally glanced at Carla and went on talking. "Josie's not so bad. People up here tend to be a little callous because of the rough lives they lead, scratching a living from the land. You get used to it after a while. My husband owned a logging company and it seemed as if the men were always having accidents—they'd cut themselves with the chain saws, or they'd break their legs. Half the time Chuck wouldn't mention it and I wouldn't find out unless I ran into the man's wife on the street. I thought he was terribly insensitive at first, but then I realized it was just a way of life. If you cut down trees for a living you expect a few nicks and bruises." They walked on in silence for a while and then she added, "Chuck was killed when the brakes went out on a logging truck he was driving."

"I'm sorry."

"It happens." Sally's voice was rough, denying the look of pain in her eyes.

"I'm surprised that Josie was so rude to Bronwin Stauffer," Carla said in an effort to get off the subject. "I can understand why Pat doesn't like the idea of an electronics plant. Her hotel depends on the tourist trade, and she wants the town to stay small and quaint. But Josie should have been pleased. A factory will mean more business for the First National."

"It's important to Josie to maintain the status quo. She likes to think she runs this town. Everybody tries to stay in good with her so they can get a loan from her husband's bank if they need one. Josie adores the feeling of power. Bronwin might take some of her power away.

"I've met Owen, Bronwin's husband," Sally went on. "He's been coming up here for the deer hunting for the last couple of years. He's quite a guy. He started his company with a good idea and a credit card loan and now he's worth millions. And he isn't one of those computer nerds, either, glued to the computer screen. He's a lot of fun. Bronwin's a lucky woman."

Carla glanced at her in surprise. Even as self-absorbed as she was these days, Sally's last remark had been wistful enough to catch her attention. Watching Sally flit from man to man at the Chamber of Commerce dance, she'd gotten the impression that she was looking for a new husband. Was she interested in Owen Stauffer? It sounded as if she was half in love with him.

Sally caught her eye and blushed. She changed the subject. "That's Maud Rucker's house." She pointed up a side street at a gaunt Victorian, a reminder of mortality among the neat stucco bungalows that surrounded it. Scraps of tired white paint peeled from the gray weathered boards and several of the porch uprights were missing. The yard was untended, the bushes overgrown and the flowerbeds filled with weeds.

As they looked at the house, a young man came out the front door. He was tall and strongly built, his trousers crusted with mud. A three days' growth of black beard gave him a furtive look. He turned when he reached the sidewalk and walked rapidly down the street in the opposite direction.

"Who was that?" Carla asked.

"Steve Rucker. He's one of the young people Maud is so afraid might leave town to find a career." Sally's voice was heavy with irony. "Steve's her great-nephew. He grew up in the East, but he came out here on a visit a few years ago and ended up by moving in with her. He claims to be a gold miner, but I think he's just a bum. Don't tell Maud I said so, though. She's devoted to him."

It had been an irritating afternoon and Carla was ready enough to join her companion in making snide remarks. "I don't suppose an electronics plant would offer him many opportunities for advancement. He wouldn't look right in a white lab coat."

"Still, it will be a great thing for Placer Bar if Owen does move his factory here." Sally sighed. "I might apply for a job myself. My husband left me enough money so I don't have to work, but it gets boring sitting around the house all day."

Carla had a suspicion that Sally was more interested in getting close to Owen Stauffer than in finding a way to occupy her time, but she decided to take the statement at face value. "I know what you mean. That's why I go fishing. It drives my husband crazy—he keeps urging me to find other interests. Maybe I should ask Owen for a job. I'm a building appraiser by profession, but there isn't much demand for that sort of skill in this town, and the locals keep what work there is for themselves." This was a sore point with her and she was unable to keep the bitter note out of her voice.

Sally's steps slowed and she came to a halt in front of a new yellow ranch house. "This is where I live. I tell you what, the next time you're at a loose end, why don't you stop by for coffee? I'm in the phone book if you want to call ahead."

Carla smiled vaguely, reluctant to make plans. "I'll call you," she said, turning away quickly to avoid committing to a specific date.

As she continued on home, Carla's thoughts turned again to Peter and their crumbling marriage. Their troubles were all her fault. She was betraying her husband with her fishing expeditions as surely as if she was carrying on with another man. Peter wasn't angry because she'd been neglecting the housework and shopping. No, he was upset because she had withdrawn from him. She was no longer functioning as his wife.

Then the bad thoughts kicked in, like a refrigerator motor when the ice threatens to melt. Peter was responsible for this mess. He'd run out on her first.

Everything had been fine when they lived in San Francisco. Then his company, Cal-Equity Savings, opened a branch in Placer Bar and sent Peter to the Sierras to run it. Peter was good at his job. He managed their new branches, establishing a solid customer base, and then moved on after a few years once he had the branch running smoothly. But this year a recession had hit and the savings and loan industry was in big trouble. Cal-Equity was losing money and the Placer Bar office was a drain on its assets. Nobody could have made a success of the branch, but that didn't make any difference. Top management blamed Peter and, what was worse, he blamed himself. He'd become driven, obsessed with his work, determined to make the branch profitable even though a profit was impossible in the current economic climate.

Peter had never failed before, and the experience had had a disastrous effect on his character. The smart, funny man she'd married in San Francisco had become a bore, obsessed with drumming up business at meetings of the local Rotary Club. To add to their troubles, he was beginning to think like the men he was associating with, for the most part a bunch of unreconstructed male chauvinists. She hadn't been kidding when she'd told Sally that she hadn't been able to find work as a building appraiser. In Placer Bar, about the only professions open to women were nursing and teaching school. The idea of a female building appraiser was considered laughable.

Carla felt sorry for Peter, but he'd become impossible to live with. What really bothered her was that he denied their problems were serious. He kept insisting that their life would return to normal once he started making money for his company again.

Carla wasn't so sure. She loved her husband, but she was

beginning to think that she shouldn't have married a banker. He was so conservative! He seemed to confuse facade with substance, putting way too much importance on their image as a successful young couple. He couldn't understand that people had to act a little strangely sometimes, do things not strictly regarded as constructive—like spending all day, every day, hiking and fishing the creek.

As she turned onto their street, she saw that Peter's Nissan was parked in front of the small tract house they'd rented. He was home already. Resolving to make more of an effort, she summoned a smile as she let herself in the door.

"How was the party?" Peter looked up from his newspaper as she walked into the living room.

"Interesting." She flopped down in the chair facing him. "Do you know a man named Owen Stauffer?"

"I've heard of him. He's a big wheel from Sacramento, owns a company called Stauffer Electronics. I understand that he's spending the summer here."

"His wife was at Josie's party. She said he's thinking of moving his electronics plant to Placer Bar."

"What? He's bringing the factory here?" Peter was electrified by her information. He jumped to his feet, his eyes blazing with excitement.

"Maybe. It sounds like the deal is still in the planning stages." Carla was taken aback by the look of desperate hope on Peter's face. "But he must be fairly serious. They've bought a house, and it's a long commute to Sacramento." She told him about Bronwin's plans for the old Kettering mansion.

"God, this is wonderful." Peter started to pace around the living room. "An electronics factory would be the making of my savings and loan."

He strode to the window and stood looking out into the

24

street. "It seemed like such a good idea, opening a branch here." His voice had grown questioning, as if he were talking to himself. "Last winter, construction was at an all-time high and the lumber business was booming. Everybody had money in their pockets; even the farmers weren't complaining. Then interest rates went up and it all fell to pieces. People are lucky if they can scrape together enough cash to make it through the month." He turned to her and smacked a fist into the palm of his hand. "Owen has *got* to bring his factory here."

It wasn't lost on Carla that Peter was going to be bitterly disappointed if the factory fell through. She was sorry now that she'd mentioned it.

Peter sat down on the arm of her chair and seized her hands, talking with a sort of desperate energy. "Everything will be fine once the electronics plant opens. I'll get the branch pulled into shape and then I'll ask for a transfer. We'll go back to San Francisco."

This was a new idea. "San Francisco! I thought you had to go where they sent you."

He shook his head. "You aren't happy here. When we first got married, you had a lot of friends—I almost resented the fact that you knew so many people. But things have been different since we moved to the mountains. You've turned into a recluse. You wander the streams with your fishing pole as if you're hiding from the human race."

"We've both been a little demoralized lately."

He squeezed her hands firmly. "It's this town. We'll feel better once we get back to the city."

"It would be wonderful if you could swing it." Carla was beginning to catch some of his enthusiasm. Maybe they *could* straighten out their marriage if they went back to San Francisco, she reflected. Then she warned herself to be reasonable. What if the factory failed to materialize?

Peter didn't seem to have any doubts. "I've done a lot for Cal-Equity over the years. If I ask for a San Francisco branch, they'll just have to give me one.

"Stauffer Electronics!" Peter sprang to his feet. "I know. Let's go for a drive. We can take a look at the old Kettering mansion, this ruined house the Stauffers are planning to fix up. Somebody was talking about the place the other day. I think I know where to find it."

Carla experienced a sinking sensation. She couldn't help feeling that Peter was putting all his eggs in the wrong basket. But she couldn't very well refuse to go. She grabbed a light jacket from the hall closet and followed him out to the car.

Chapter 3

Carla and Peter drove down Broad Street, then turned left on Ridge Road past an old cemetery, The Blue and the Gray. This burial ground dated from the Civil War and was no longer much used. Union supporters were buried on the left side of the path and Confederate sympathizers on the right. Carla had spent an afternoon looking at the grass-grown marble headstones, many of them set in family plots bordered by rocks or iron railings. She'd noticed that the graves dating from the 1860's and 1870's were divided fairly evenly between the two sides. Later on, the graves were concentrated in the Union burial ground until it came to the 1950's, when a number of modern headstones had been put up in the Confederate section. She had an idea this didn't show a sudden upsurge of support for the South, but indicated a loss of interest in the old conflict. People buried their dead where they could find room.

The houses thinned out beyond the cemetery, with only the occasional tarpaper-patched cabin or rusty trailer to show they were near a town. Most of the dwellings had old cars parked out front and piles of junk in their front yards, and all the houses had the sad, scabby look of a country slum. This was the poorest part of Placer Bar, the place people moved when they couldn't afford to live anywhere else. It seemed an unlikely neighborhood in which to find Bronwin Stauffer.

They rounded a last curve and came to two stone pillars smothered in ivy. The iron gates were rusted open and one of them leaned at an angle. An enormous station wagon was parked on the road near the gates. Carla was used to Peter's Nissan and this General Motors product impressed her as swollen, almost monstrous looking in its size.

"This must be the place," she said. "That's just the sort of car I'd expect Bronwin to drive. That station wagon is a landed gentry status symbol."

Peter parked behind it and they walked through the gates. Carla drew in her breath when she caught sight of the house.

It was an antebellum-style Southern plantation mansion complete with huge wooden pillars, three proud stories with spreading low wings on either side. Scarlett O'Hara would have felt right at home. Carla was amazed; more than that, she was instantly captivated. There were plenty of old buildings in California's Sierra foothills, but they were ordinary Victorians. This was something altogether different.

They crunched up the long gravel drive toward the house, avoiding the small bushes that had taken root and blocked the way for cars. The illusion of beauty faded as they drew closer; the building took on the withdrawn and covert look of a house that has stood empty for too long. The cheap plywood covering the front windows had warped away from the frames and spray-painted grafitti defaced the easily reachable part of the facade. It was heartbreaking, Carla reflected, like seeing a gentle old lady humiliated by a rude clerk in a store.

Then she realized that the front door was standing open.

"Let's go inside," she urged, mesmerized.

"What? We can't go barging into someone else's house."

"Oh, come on. The Stauffers must be checking over their new property. I've met Bronwin Stauffer and I can introduce you." Without waiting for an answer, she ran up the stairs. Peter hesitated in the driveway for a moment and then followed her.

She rapped on the side of the door frame as she walked in. "Anybody home?"

A man emerged from the drawing room to the left of the front hall. He was wearing a business suit, but he carried a hammer in one hand and cobwebs dirtied the sleeve of his fine light wool jacket. "I'm Owen Stauffer. Can I help you with something?"

So this was Bronwin's husband, Carla thought. He wasn't the handsome heartbreaker Sally's behavior had led her to expect. Owen was a pleasant-faced man in his late thirties, of medium height, with a furry mustache and furry short brown hair. His forehead was heavily lined, giving him a perplexed look, as if he spent a lot of time wondering just where he'd left the car keys.

Peter stepped forward. "I'm Peter Weber and this is my wife, Carla. She met your wife this afternoon at Josie Kettering's tea party."

"We came by to take a look at the house and we noticed that the door was open," Carla explained. "We thought we'd make sure nothing was wrong."

"Wrong?" Owen repeated, glancing ruefully around the room. Even in the dim light from the doorway it was obvious that the house was a mess. Faded wallpaper hung down in spirals from the ceiling, the plaster under the windows was crumbling where rain had gotten in, and the parquet floor was stained and buckled. Thick layers of dirty gray paint gave the staircase an institutional look.

"Carla tells me you're planning to restore the house." Peter's voice was unctuous, syrupy with false charm.

Carla jerked away and stared at her husband in disbelief.

29

She could have kicked him for his ingratiating tone. Peter had never talked that way to *anyone* in San Francisco. This was a horrible new development.

Fortunately, Owen didn't seem to notice. "My wife wants to turn the clock back, do a historically accurate restoration job. I'm not sure it's such a good idea, but I know I'm going to like living in the foothills. I've had it with Sacramento; it's hot and dry and dusty and the traffic is terrible. It's an overgrown small town, with all the problems of a city and none of the advantages.

"Come on up and meet Bronwin," he added, leading the way upstairs.

They trailed through several rooms, all large and beautifully proportioned. Carla made herself stop thinking about Peter's eagerness to ingratiate himself with Owen. She looked around eagerly, seeing beyond the broken plaster and the dingy woodwork to the true beauty of the house. This place was magnificent, she told herself, looking up to admire a decorative plaster ceiling rosette. She experienced a sudden overwhelming pang of envy as she realized that it belonged to the Stauffers.

Bronwin hadn't impressed her as the type to see value in the history of a building. Carla had a good idea that the Stauffers had bought the house because it was big and Bronwin liked the imposing pillars and she'd heard that restoring old mansions was fashionable. This house deserved a better owner. It should have gone to someone who could truly appreciate it, she thought longingly. Someone like her.

Carla realized that she was falling in love with the house.

They found Bronwin in the master bedroom, which was empty except for some debris on the floor and an open toolbox. She was standing in front of a window, using a magnifying glass to examine a chunk of molding that had fallen off the door. She looked up and nodded in an abstracted way when Carla introduced Peter.

"Darling, I think I've discovered the original color of this woodwork." She turned to Owen, holding out the piece of trim. "What do you think? The bottom layer of paint seems to be a pale gray."

Carla gave her a look of disgust. This woman obviously knew nothing about old houses. Of course, she hadn't had Carla's experience working with the people who renovated them, she was forced to admit.

"I think you're mistaken," she said, reaching out and taking the chunk of molding from Bronwin's hand. "Mind if I try something?"

Carla placed the fragment of wood on the floor, then grabbed a chisel from the toolbox and commandeered Owen's hammer. She chipped a wide, shallow gouge in the painted side and examined it carefully through Bronwin's magnifying glass.

"The gray is a base coat." She handed the piece of molding back to Bronwin. "The original paint is that magenta you see over the gray."

"How can you tell?" Bronwin looked at her with real interest for the first time.

"There's a thin line of dirt on top of the magenta. There's nothing between the magenta and the gray, and that means the gray paint wasn't left exposed for very long."

"How clever! Where'd you learn to do that?"

"I worked as a building appraiser before we moved to Placer Bar. I picked up the odd bit of information."

"You know, I could use some help with this place." Bronwin looked at her with a speculative expression. "I'm planning to do a really authentic restoration job, but I don't have much time for research. Would you be interested in giving me a hand?

I need someone to go over the house and identify the original wall treatments, maybe even keep an eye on the contractor to make sure he does his job properly."

Carla recoiled, cut to her very core. Bronwin was asking her to make this house beautiful for her and Owen? It was as if Bronwin had asked to borrow one of her dresses so she could flirt with Carla's lover. "You'd better find someone else," she said stiffly. "I'm not an expert at this sort of thing. Besides, I'm awfully busy right now."

Bronwin's lips tightened in a smile. She was taking Carla's refusal as a challenge. Bronwin looked at Peter, sizing him up and concluding that he was the one to help her get her way.

"You probably think I'm foolish to want to restore this old place," she told him, lowering her eyes. "Your wife clearly isn't interested in my pet project."

"Of course she is. I'm sure she'll be delighted to help." Peter gave Carla a near-desperate look. She responded with a glare of fury. So he wanted to make friends with the Stauffers— big deal! How could he be so disloyal to her?

Owen interrupted at this point. "We'd take it as a favor, and of course we'd expect to pay you. How much do you charge? Or would you prefer to wait and give us a quote when you've decided how much effort will be involved?"

Carla was about to tell him to forget it, but then she looked around the room. She could imagine it as it would look when the construction work was finished, with a fire in the marble fireplace and lamplight reflected in the tall sash windows. The way it would look if it were *her* bedroom. It dawned on her that if she took the job, it would give her an excuse to spend time in this house. The place would be hers, for a week or two at least, while she did the research.

She made one last half-hearted effort to escape. "It's a wonderful opportunity, and I'm grateful, but couldn't you find someone better qualified?"

"We've tried," Bronwin said bluntly. "I talked to a man who worked on restoring the Capitol Building in Sacramento. He said the Kettering mansion was an interesting anomaly, but it wasn't architecturally significant enough to make it worth his time."

This woman was going to make a horrible employer. Carla remembered Bronwin's remark about a "captive labor force" at Josie's party. But she and Peter could use the extra money, and the house itself was a strong inducement to accept. It would break her heart if Bronwin made a botch of the restoration job. She hesitated, and Peter rushed in to fill the gap. "Carla would be delighted to help," he said, taking her firmly by the arm.

"Then it's settled," Bronwin told him. "We won't expect Carla to work full time, but we'd appreciate it if she could get started as soon as possible. We're bringing in some workmen next week to handle a few of the rough jobs, like replacing the roof."

Owen reached into his pocket and produced a spare set of keys. He handed them to Carla. The iron keys felt heavy in her grasp, cold and exciting to the touch.

"We've rented a house to live in until the mansion is ready," Bronwin went on briskly. She handed her a business card embossed with a phone number and an address at Mother Lode Lake, a luxury development on the edge of town. "Give me a call if you run into any problems or if you make any exciting discoveries. I'll want to keep in close touch with your progress."

Oh, hell, Carla told herself, realizing that the situation had gotten out of control. She was working for Bronwin now, there were no two ways about it. This was all Peter's fault.

Peter didn't have much to say on the drive home. He finally

spoke as they were walking across the lawn to their front door. "I guess I pushed you into taking that job. I'm sorry if I made things awkward. But maybe you'll enjoy it. Bronwin should be easy to work with, at any rate. She seems like a pleasant sort of person."

"You can't be serious! She's the most obnoxious woman I've met in a long while."

Carla looked at her husband sadly. What were they coming to? She'd taken refuge in escapism, becoming a compulsive fisherman, and thwarted ambition seemed to have made Peter soft in the head.

The thought of their shared unhappy plight filled her with warmth, a sense of fellow-feeling. "Oh, well," she went on more gently. "The project won't last forever. I guess I can put up with Bronwin for a short while."

"Make an effort to get along with her, for my sake," Peter begged, suddenly anxious. "Owen is going to be an important man in this town if he brings the factory here. I can't afford to have you feuding with his wife."

"You should have thought of that before you got me into this mess," she told him, enjoying the expression on his face. "If there's trouble, you have only yourself to blame."

Then she took pity on him. "Let's get some rest," she said, unlocking the door. "I have a new job to start in the morning and I want to be fresh."

Chapter 4

Carla woke up the next day in a surprisingly cheerful mood. It felt good to be working again. She hummed to herself as she toasted frozen waffles for breakfast and when it was time for Peter to leave, her goodbye kiss expressed genuine affection.

As she watched him back the car down the drive, it occurred to her that this was the first time in months that she hadn't felt resentful when he left for the office. She'd started to feel that he was abandoning, her, slipping away into a wider and more interesting world when he left the house each morning. And what must it have been like for him? she asked herself, with a sudden rush of compunction. Poor Peter, going off every day to a job that made him miserable, leaving his wife to sulk pointlessly and then flee to the woods where she could forget the life they shared together. No wonder he was always in such a lousy mood when he came home.

Well, they were through with that, for the time being. The Kettering mansion would keep her gainfully employed for the next few weeks—for months, even, if she got involved with the construction work. And if she did a good job with the restoration project, maybe it would lead to something permanent, another position in some related field. She hunted out her metal tape measure and a pad of graph paper and set out on foot for Bronwin's ruined house.

Once again, she experienced the strange sensation of coming home as she passed through the through the tall stone gates. A feeling of rightful possession stole over her as she turned her key in the lock and pushed open the front door. It was as if she were reclaiming an inheritance, a much-loved family home that she'd lost and feared never to see again.

Her heart beat with excitement as she stepped inside. Enough light seeped through the chinks of the boarded-up windows so she could see her way. She prowled the hall and the two big front parlors and the smaller side rooms that had once served as offices, when the mansion had been the owner's place of business as well as his home. She was particularly delighted by a small semicircular chamber at the rear of the building, a sun room that must have been used for informal entertaining. The remains of a mural, a fox-hunting scene, could still be made out; the faded pink coats of the hunters glowed in the dimness against a dark forest background.

The bedrooms were on the second floor, up the great staircase. The rooms all had doors opening onto the hallway, but there were also smaller connecting doors between them. The ladies of the house could have visited one another in their dressing gowns, or tended their children, while men here on business circulated downstairs. A neat division between private and public life. Or perhaps this was a measure to conserve heat, Carla reflected. Each bedroom had a fireplace, and in winter the occupants would have been reluctant to open their doors to the chilly great hall and central stairwell. Carla didn't know enough about this type of architecture to decide.

She followed a narrow flight of steps up to the third story, a rabbit warren of storerooms and servants' quarters, then returned to the second floor and sat down at the top of the grand stairs.

The thing that fascinated her about this house was not its

ruined beauty but its dignity, she reflected. It seemed to promise a wider, more generous way of life. If only they lived here, she and Peter would stop squabbling. He'd forget his preoccupation with making money and turn back into the man she'd fallen in love with. Their days would be full of warmth and light and graciousness, free of anger and betrayal.

Of course, this thought was in itself a form of treachery, she told herself with a pang of guilt. Peter wasn't a figure from a romance novel. He was a flesh and blood human being, a man who was doing his flawed best to deal with very real problems. He'd be hurt if he knew what she was thinking.

Not to mention the fact that he liked to think of her as an intelligent woman. He'd be horrified to learn that she'd taken refuge in such a silly dream, an idealized vision of a past free of difficulties. No, she told herself, she must banish these irrational thoughts.

But the house! She couldn't shake the feeling that it had something important to offer her. Some sort of solution, some sort of redemption. If only it could be her home! Surely her life would be different.

Carla pulled herself together with an effort. She was here to do a job, to earn some extra money. Rising to her feet, she reached into her backpack and took out her tape measure. Clutching its hard metal case for comfort, she walked through the house again, this time making herself look at it through the eyes of a professional.

Like most old buildings, the Kettering mansion had fallen victim to the human urge to make improvements. It had been remodeled a number of times over the years. Some of the changes were obvious, like the wallboard partitions dividing the big downstairs rooms. Other alterations might be harder to detect. Identifying the original paint colors was going to be the least of her problems, she told herself. She would have to figure out where the walls were supposed to go before she started worrying about how to cover them with paint and wallpaper.

The first thing to do was draw up a tentative floor plan. The final drawings would have to wait until the contractor's crew could help her dig into the walls to look for signs of change—the square holes left by old iron nails would show that wooden beams had been torn away, while modern materials would prove that a wall was a recent addition. But if she prepared a rough sketch, it would give her a place to start. She took out her pad of graph paper. She felt a little more grounded now that she'd formulated a practical plan of action.

Her work measuring the first floor rooms went smoothly, but she ran into a problem when she tackled the second story. The broad central hallway was three feet too short. It ended in a blank wall positioned a yard ahead of the outside walls of the adjoining bedrooms.

She must have made a mistake, she told herself. She measured again. There was no getting around it; the hallway had been cut off at the end for some reason. She rapped on the surface of the wall and her knuckles produced a hollow sound instead of the solid thump of plaster.

The hall was lined with peeling wallpaper. She grabbed a hanging corner and worked it loose, tearing the paper off to reveal two floor-length wooden doors designed to open outwards. Of course! A linen closet. But why had someone gone to the trouble of covering it up?

The door handles had been taken away so the wallpaper would fit smoothly, and the doors were sealed into their frames with what looked like dried-out glue, but she managed to hook the metal tab-end of her tape measure into a narrow crevice. She worked the tool up and down, dislodging flakes of yellow adhesive, then hauled on the tape. The right-hand door splintered open.

She was looking at a dead body, or at least the remains of one. It was lying on a shelf about four feet off the floor. The corpse's eyes were sunk deep into the wrinkles of the leather-covered skull. The thin lips were drawn back in a snarl and the exposed brown teeth leered at her horribly. A full head of improbably healthy-looking long black hair and a black goatee added to the menace of the apparition.

Carla was so surprised that she went numb at first. Then she screamed. Galvanized by superstitious terror, she dropped the tape measure and bolted down the hall.

She ran down the stairs and was halfway to the front door before she recovered her reason. She couldn't have seen what she thought she'd seen, she told herself as she forced her steps to a halt. The creature was a hallucination, a horrible hallucination. It couldn't have really been there.

Her steps dragging with reluctance, she went back up the stairs and down the hall to the linen closet. The dead man was still lying on the shelf, waiting for her. She pulled open the left-side door so she could view him in his entirety. The shriveled body was clothed in patched leather trousers and a military-style jacket with yellow cuffs and collar and gold braid on the sleeves. He lounged on his side on the broad middle shelf of the otherwise empty closet. Worn black boots covered the creature's feet.

She squeezed her eyes shut, then opened them. The man in the brown military jacket refused to disappear. It occurred to her that he was her enemy, an evil spirit that had materialized in an effort to force its way into her world. The shriveled skull face stared at her with a sly, duplicitous expression, and the sunken eyes seemed to hold a challenging gleam.

Carla still didn't believe that she'd found a mummified dead body in the linen closet. But, on the other hand, it was hard to convince herself that she hadn't. This apparition was even more irrational than her idea that the house would miraculously solve her problems with Peter. Things had reached the point where she couldn't rely on the evidence of her own senses. She had never felt so low in her life.

She abandoned herself to torpor for a few minutes, standing slumped against the wall. Then her mind started clicking over again. Okay, she'd found a dead body. What did you do with dead bodies? You called the police.

And that was what she would do, she resolved. She didn't care if her imagination was playing tricks on her. She was going to report this situation to the authorities. If all she accomplished was to alert them to her own extremely doubtful mental condition, so be it.

It was a relief to take decisive action. Closing her mind to the possible consequences, the shame of reporting an imaginary crime complete with an imaginary dead body, she left the house and strode briskly to the highway. She located a pay phone at the Conoco station about half a mile from the house.

"Homicide, please," she told the cop who answered the call. She noticed with detached pride that her voice was businesslike and level.

"What do you think this is, New York City?" the man answered. "This is the Placer Bar Police Station. We aren't anywhere big enough to have a homicide department." He chuckled for a moment and then stopped abruptly. "Hey, this sounds important. I'll put you through to Lieutenant Pressner."

The line went dead, then clicked alive again. A new voice snapped from the receiver. "You're calling to report a murder?"

"I've found a dead body in a sealed-off cupboard at the

Kettering mansion. The man's obviously been dead for some time."

Carla identified herself and explained about the work she'd been doing. The Lieutenant told her to meet him at the mansion and hung up.

Pride made her hesitate, but then she decided that if she was going to make a spectacle of herself by babbling about non-existent corpses, she might as well do a thorough job. She placed a call to Bronwin.

She reached the Stauffers' answering machine. "I've found a skeleton in one of your closets," she said into the receiver. "You might want to stop by the old Kettering place if you get a chance."

The cops had already reached the house by the time she got back. Lieutenant Pressner was a dark, burly man in early middle age. He was peering disapprovingly into the linen closet, his long-nosed face twisted into a frown. His assistant, a blond and pink-cheeked cop in uniform who looked as if he'd recently starred on the high school football team, stood respectfully behind him. The younger cop had the blissful expression of a man who can't believe his luck. This was clearly a red letter day for him, the sort of exciting adventure he'd joined the police to find.

To Carla's inexpressible relief, the two cops seemed to be having no trouble accepting the body as real. Lieutenant Pressner was actually prodding the creature's face with his fingers. She shuddered.

The Lieutenant nodded, acknowledging her presence. "He was shot, ma'am," he announced. "You can see the exit wound right here." He lifted the body's head a little to show the remains of dried blood on the side of the skull. Some of the corpse's long black hair came off in his hands.

"Yes, I knew it must have been murder. He couldn't have sealed himself into the closet without help." Carla realized that she was chattering inanely, but she didn't care. She was overwhelmed with relief to learn that she wasn't in the grip of a delusion.

Pressner noticed that she was distraught, although he misunderstood the cause. "Of course, this happened a long time ago," he said soothingly. "There's no need to be frightened. The killer is long gone."

Brisk footsteps tapped across the floor. They turned to see Bronwin striding toward them down the hall. "Carla, what did you mean by that cryptic message? The one you left on my answering machine?"

Then her eyes went past them to the corpse. "Yeep!" she cried. Her mouth dropped open and her body recoiled, seeming to fold in on itself.

"Maybe you ladies should wait downstairs." Lieutenant Pressner's voice was solicitous. "He isn't a pretty sight."

"I'm all right," Bronwin said, although she obviously hadn't recovered. She took a shaky step forward. "My God, I was looking for local color when I bought this house, but I guess I got more than I bargained for," she joked feebly.

Carla had no intention of leaving, either. Now that her doubts about the corpse's reality were settled, she was consumed with curiosity. "Who was he?" she demanded, finally taking in the enormity of the crime that had happened here. "And who could have killed him?"

"We may have some trouble answering those questions. I don't recognize his face, but judging from that fancy jacket he's wearing, I'd say he was one of the hippies that used this house as a crash pad back in the Seventies. Look at his long hair and beard." Lieutenant Pressner's face took on a look of gloomy satisfaction. "I always said that bunch would come to no good."

"You mean we've got an anonymous corpse on our hands?" For some reason, the idea that the body didn't have a name upset Carla terribly.

"I doubt if we'll get usable prints off those fingers." The Lieutenant pointed at the shriveled claw that was all that remained of the corpse's left hand. "And if we do, there's no guarantee that his prints are on file, especially after all this time. Of course, with any luck, some witness will come forward and identify him. We won't have any trouble getting publicity. The media will have a field day with this one."

Carla was still clutching her tape measure. Pressner took it and skated the tape out alongside the body in a grotesque parody of her room-measuring technique. "Say, this is interesting. The guy was unusually short, about five-foot two or three, I'd say. That should help us with the identification."

Then his voice took on a cautious note. "Actually, I'd appreciate it if you ladies wouldn't mention his height. We always want to withhold a few facts from the public in an investigation like this one."

"What do you mean?" Bronwin demanded.

"Just that we're going to get a lot of calls when this hits the papers, most of them from cranks. If the caller wants to tell us about a tall man, we'll know we can safely ignore the information." He shook his head doubtfully. "This case is twenty years old, at the very least. If I'm going to have a hope in hell of solving it, I've got to find out who the victim was."

"You're making it sound as if you don't expect to catch the murderer!" Carla said accusingly.

"You've got to understand, it could have been anyone. This house was a sort of regional crash pad for over ten years. There must have been hundreds of hippies who lived here during that period. Some of them stayed for a long time, months or even years, but others only dropped by for a short visit. If the killer was just passing through—" He shrugged. "Our man here could have been murdered by a traveling companion, and nobody would remember either of them after this lapse of time."

"But—" Carla broke off in mid-objection. She hated to admit it, but the Lieutenant's argument made sense. Who would remember a stranger met casually twenty years ago?

"Twenty years or more," she contented herself with saying. "It's amazing he's so well preserved."

"Yes, well." Pressner gave her a kindly look. "I've read about this sort of thing in *National Geographic*. Corpses turn to leather if they're kept dry and there's enough air circulation. That's why the ancient Egyptians started mummifying their dead. They'd bury their companions in the desert and come back years later to find their bodies preserved by the sand. They decided that was the way it was supposed to be, and they developed a whole science around the phenomenon, inventing embalming to improve on the process." He held up a cautionary finger. "Of course, when I said twenty years, it was just a guess. We'll have to bring in a forensic pathologist to give us an accurate date of death."

Carla turned back toward the body. Now that she was getting used to him, the dead man's face had lost its crafty look. Instead he seemed sad, even pitiable. His left arm was flung to the side, the fingers curled upward as if imploring her help.

"You know, maybe I could give you a hand with this case," she said impulsively. "Bronwin hired me to research the early history of the house, but there's no reason I couldn't look into the hippie period, too. I could ask a few questions around town—" She glanced at Bronwin for approval.

"No! Definitely not!" Lieutenant Pressner's small dark eyes flashed with alarm. "You've got to understand something, ma'am. The murderer may still live in Placer Bar. He—or she—is not going to be happy to hear that the body has been discovered. If you were to start in snooping, you could put your-self in grave danger." He smoothed back his thinning black hair. "No, you've done your duty by reporting this to the police. It's our problem now.

"What I'd like you to do is give your statements to Bob, here," the Lieutenant went on. "He'll drive you to the police station." He nodded at the young blond cop, whose face split in a delighted grin at the prospect of hearing all the gory details. "Then you ladies can go home. I'll be bringing in a forensic team and I'll have to close off the house for a day or two while they do their work."

The corpse had been caught up in the bureaucratic machinery. What a fate for what had once been a man! Sighing regretfully, Carla picked up her backpack and followed the blond cop downstairs.

Chapter 5

Lieutenant Pressner was quick to publicize the discovery of the murder. The Sacramento TV channel carried a picture of the dead man on the evening news, a photograph of the corpse stretched out on the linen closet shelf. They also showed an artist's sketch of the victim as he might have looked when still alive. According to the police artist he'd been an attractive fellow, in his early twenties at the oldest, with a broad forehead and a strong chin. Carla found his youthful good looks heartbreaking. He might have been the boyfriend of the purple-haired girl who'd acted as the maid at Josie's party.

Carla had asked Pressner to play down her role as much as possible, and she was glad to see that he'd kept her name out of the news. The last thing she wanted was to have some reporter asking her how she'd felt when she found the body.

Especially since Peter was being so unreasonable. "What are you trying to do, drive the Stauffers out of town?" he'd yelled. "You confronted poor Bronwin with a moldering corpse? A dead body you'd dragged out of the wall of her very own house? That's disgusting! I wouldn't be surprised if she and Owen didn't decide to pack up and leave Placer Bar forever."

"What did you expect me to do? Tuck the body discreetly into the garbage can and hope the trash collectors wouldn't notice? I didn't have a whole lot of choice in the matter."

"Well, you didn't have to leave a message on Bronwin's answering machine. It would have been a whole lot better if she hadn't actually seen the body." He thought for a moment, rubbing his jaw, and then his eyes widened in accusation again. "Hey, did the damn thing *stink?*"

"No." She gave him a quelling look.

Peter was still in a bad mood at the breakfast table the next morning. He picked up a piece of toast, looked at it, and dropped it back on his plate. "Any chance of some eggs?"

"I'll fix you eggs if you want them. Yesterday you were worried about cholesterol." Carla got up from the kitchen table and started cracking eggs into the skillet.

"I need a substantial breakfast to face the day. Something bad is going to happen, I can just feel it. My biggest depositor will take his money out, or an important loan will fall through. Maybe the prime rate will go up again and I won't be able to lend any money at all."

"I thought our troubles were over. Remember? We're moving back to San Francisco if the new plant comes through."

"That's a big 'if'. Even if Owen isn't put off by your finding a dead body, he'll have to buy land, get building permits—a dozen things could go wrong. And even if he pulls it all together, the factory will probably come too late to help me. Headquarters will have closed down the branch by then, or they'll have fired me and put in a new manager.

"That's the way it will go," he continued with gloomy satisfaction. "Some new guy will take over just before the plant opens. He'll get the credit for making the branch a success and I'll have a bad name in the industry."

Carla didn't reply. She shoveled his eggs onto a plate. He ate a few bites and left the house, complaining that she'd made him late for work.

47

She sighed and put the dishes in the sink. The air in the house was stale and oppressive; it seemed like the walls were closing in on her. She couldn't visit the Kettering mansion since it was cordoned off with police tape, but there was still her old refuge, Casitas Creek, the stream that ran through their town. Leaving the dishes unrinsed and the bed unmade, she grabbed her fishing pole and the rest of her gear and practically ran out the door.

She couldn't find a stretch of water that suited her, or maybe she was just restless. She walked for several miles before she found a spot that she liked. Huge boulders formed a gorge through which the stream poured in a sheet of white foam. Below the shallow waterfall was a green pool, shaded by pine trees. The creek curved close by the highway here, but the splashing water masked the sound of traffic.

She sat down on the sun warmed stream bank and threw out her line, allowing the orange salmon egg she was using as bait to be carried off by the rushing water. As she'd planned, it drifted to a relatively still spot protected by a rock, the sort of place where a fish might wait to catch its dinner as the food washed by. She hooked a trout almost immediately, a big one from the feel of it. She gave a yelp of excitement and jumped to her feet, oblivious to her surroundings as she always was when she caught a fish. It was a perfect moment, separate from the rest of her life.

She reeled her catch to the shallows and bent over to unhook it. "Hey!" The voice came from behind her.

She lost her balance and almost toppled into the creek. Grabbing a bush to steady herself, she straightened up and turned around, the fish still clutched in one hand. A young man stood about five feet away, glaring at her. He was dressed in worn blue jeans and a work shirt, and his untidy dark hair stood on end as if he'd been swimming and had dried it with a towel. A dark growth of stubble added to the menace of his expression.

It took her a moment, but then she remembered where she'd seen him before. He was Steve Rucker, Maud's nephew, the man Sally had pointed out the other day.

"What are you doing here?" he demanded.

"Fishing, obviously." She felt a little intimidated and this made her angry.

"Well, do it somewhere else. I don't like people hanging around this part of the river."

Why was Steve trying to bully her? Was every man she talked to today going to push her around? "This is government land," she informed him. "I have as much right to be here as you do."

"Actually, it's private property and you're both trespassing." A man in a blue business suit approached them from the road. To Carla's relief, it was Owen Stauffer.

Then she realized what he was doing here, dressed for the office. "Owen! This must be where you're planning to build the factory."

He gave her a funny look and she started to talk nervously. "This is a great spot for it. If you clear away a few trees you'll have a level lot to build on, and it's always nice to be by the water." She cleared her throat. "Plus you've got access to the road."

"Wait a minute—you're going to put a factory here?" Steve Rucker broke in on their conversation. "You can't do that! I have a claim on this part of the river."

"It can't be registered," Owen told him. "This area is privately owned. I'm negotiating to buy the land, in fact."

"It's the Code of the West." Steve glared at him ferociously. "If a man has a claim, he doesn't need a bunch of papers to protect his rights. We have our own way of dealing with claim jumpers around here."

"The Code of the West?" Owen repeated. He sounded bemused.

"You heard me." Steve's voice had grown high and squeaky; he was finding his tough-guy act hard to keep up. He hesitated, then whirled and crashed off through the underbrush.

"What was that all about?" Owen spread his hands, appealing to Carla.

"His name is Steve Rucker. He's some sort of amateur prospector from the East, I've heard. I guess he thinks he's found gold along here."

"That isn't very likely. Thousands of people have panned this river and if there was any gold to find, they'd have taken it out long ago."

Owen glanced toward the road again, losing interest, but Carla knew that Peter would never forgive her if she didn't ask him about his business plans. "Have you actually made an offer on this property? It sounds as if you're really going to move your factory to Placer Bar."

"That decision is contingent on a lot of factors." He smiled evasively. "The man who owns this land is asking more than I want to pay, and I'll have to submit an environmental impact report. I'm not sure what I'm going to do."

Carla understood. Like so many people in the middle of a real estate negotiation, Owen didn't want to talk about it for fear of losing bargaining power. He disengaged himself and headed down the path before she could think of anything to say. In a minute, she heard his car engine revving up.

Still, his words had been promising. She was sure he *wanted* to put the factory here. And if Owen was half as clever as people seemed to think he was, he'd probably find a way to do it.

Sighing, she knelt and gathered up her fishing gear. She decided to leave before Steve Rucker returned. The encounter with Maud's nephew had destroyed her mood for fishing.

Back home, she cleaned the trout she'd caught and put it in the refrigerator. She stored her fishing gear in the guest room closet where she kept it out of Peter's way. She cleared away the breakfast things and straightened the bedroom, then wandered aimlessly into the living room. Now that the Kettering mansion was off-limits, how was she going to spend the rest of the day?

She snapped her fingers as she remembered that Sally Bolt had asked her to drop by for coffee. She decided to take her up on the invitation—and she'd take her the newly-caught fish. Carla went back into the kitchen and looked up the telephone number in the directory.

Sally seemed pleased to hear from her. "Sure, today would be perfect. I was thinking of straightening out the garage, but I'm always glad to have an excuse to put off that particular job."

Sally was dressed casually in khaki slacks and a bandanna-print shirt when she answered the door, but she was wearing her usual heavy eye makeup. She seemed a little surprised when she peeked inside the paper bag Carla handed her and saw the trout, but she quickly recovered her aplomb and stowed the fish in the refrigerator.

The house was a large one, three or four bedrooms, Carla guessed. The kitchen was huge, with two big plant-stuffed greenhouse windows. A long counter and a row of hanging cabinets separated the kitchen from a breakfast room. This was comfortably crammed with furniture, a circular pine breakfast table plus a desk stuffed with correspondence, and an easy chair faced a bookcase with a small television set on top of it. A book lay face-down on the chair and Carla got the impression that Sally spent a lot of her time here. She even kept some of her clothing on a rack near the side door; a beige raincoat, a couple of sweaters and what looked like a man's wheat-colored corduroy jacket.

Sally heated up some croissants from the local bakery and made a fresh pot of coffee. Predictably, she used a designer roast of bean and brewed the coffee much too strong. Carla hovered by the stove while her hostess worked, and when the food was ready they carried their pottery mugs to the breakfast table.

Carla took a bite of her pastry, dabbing flaky crumbs from the tabletop with a paper napkin. "I ran into Steve Rucker this morning while I was fishing," she offered. "Owen Stauffer was there, too. They got into an argument about a plot of land near the creek. Owen is thinking of buying it for his factory, but Steve seems to think he has a gold claim there."

Sally's eyes had grown bright with interest when Carla mentioned Owen. Now she turned down the edges of her mouth in disgust. "Jeez, I knew Steve was green, but he must be a real idiot if he thinks he's going to find gold in Casitas Creek."

"There must be some gold in the river," Carla argued. "I'm always running into kids who are panning for the stuff."

"Sure, they do it as a hobby, but all they get for their trouble is a few little specks. They'd make more money working at McDonald's. Casitas Creek is panned out.

"All the easy gold was taken out during the gold rush," Sally went on. "Placer Bar is a small town now, with less than a thousand residents, but back in 1850 the population was ten times as big. That's how the creek got its name—the prospectors camped out on tiny claims along the water, with only a few bits of wood or a scrap of canvas to shelter them from the elements. A group of Spanish trappers came by and laughed at the 'little houses' or 'casitas'. Anyway, the miners came here determined to make their fortunes and they really worked hard. They must have washed every shovelful of earth several times over, and they got almost all the river gold out in a couple of years. Those old fellows were hungry. They didn't leave much for people like Steve Rucker."

"So gold isn't part of the local economy anymore?"

"I didn't say that," Sally protested. "People still do hardrock mining, burrowing into the ground and taking out ore. They've done that for many years. You've probably heard that they're reopening the Ebbets Mine as a tourist attraction? That's just one of the abandoned diggings running under Placer Bar. You need money for hardrock mining, though; money and heavy equipment."

"Peter was telling me about the Ebbets Mine. He said the mine opening was going to be the highlight of the Pioneer Days celebration. I didn't realize the tunnel ran under the town itself, though." Carla blinked, taken aback. She envisioned the tunnel giving way, the ground slowly cracking open, people screaming as houses and cars fell into a deep hole. Then a great cloud of dust mushrooming up in the silence that followed the terrible mine collapse.

Sally looked at her in amusement, reading her thoughts. "Don't worry. It's safe enough. They're installing new braces and everything. They have to, if they're going to keep the tourists happy when they ride down the shaft on the reproduction mining carts. Actually, most of the land under this town is honeycombed with old tunnels. The Ebbets Mine was one of the richest, though. They took out millions of dollars worth of gold before they closed the mine down, and now it's going to bring in more money when the tourists pay to take a look at it."

"Gold," Carla said thoughtfully. "As I understand it, the

Spanish controlled California until fairly late in the game, 1848 or so. What was it called when we took the state over, the War with Mexico?"

"It wasn't much of a war." Sally waved a hand dismissively. "More a succession of skirmishes. Only about sixty people got killed, three or four of them Mexican."

"I guess they wished they'd put up more of a resistance when gold was discovered. Although I've heard that even the Americans didn't believe it when they heard about the gold strike at Sutter's Mill."

"Yeah, the people back East thought the Californians were pulling a fast one, trying to con them into moving out here. It took a Presidential proclamation and Horace Greeley to convince people there really was gold in California." Sally giggled. "Serves them right for being so cynical. Those Easterners could have done well for themselves if they'd gone West in 1848 when they first heard the news."

Carla grinned and helped herself to another croissant. She was enjoying Sally's company. It had been a long time since she'd kidded around over coffee with a friend.

"What do you think of Bronwin's plan to fix up the old Kettering mansion? Josie didn't seem to like the idea. She told Bronwin she was making a big mistake."

"The Stauffers have a real project on their hands." Sally topped off their mugs from a Melitta pot. "The house was built by Howard's grandfather, Davis Kettering. Howard's parents sold it when Davis died and the place has sat there rotting ever since. It's too big for one family so it was used as a boarding house for a while, but the people who ran it didn't do much in the way of maintenance work. Eventually they left town, just abandoned the house, and a bunch of hippies moved in. It turned into a crash pad where anyone who wanted to could unroll their sleeping bag. Then the city seized it for back taxes. They were afraid somebody would fall through a rotten floorboard and sue them, so they condemned the place and boarded it up. Now only the rats live there."

Why did everyone keep talking about rats? First Josie and now Sally. Carla bristled, offended. The house needed work, sure, but it was hardly infested with vermin. Rodents are attracted by food, and it wasn't as if people had been holding picnics there.

"I suppose the house has a certain amount of historical importance," Sally went on. "I understand it's one of the oldest buildings in the area. Most of the early houses were destroyed by fire. They used oil lamps back then, and cooked with wood, so the downtown area was always going up in flames. Davis Kettering built his house out in the country and it escaped that fate."

"I'm so glad it survived! The house is irreplaceable." Carla spoke without thinking and immediately regretted her words. She knew there was something abnormal about the spell the house had cast on her. Her longing to own it and her sense that it could somehow save her from herself were irrational in the extreme. She didn't want Sally to guess how she felt.

Sally simply nodded; she hadn't noticed anything wrong. "Davis Kettering was terribly proud of his house, I've heard. He lived there until the day he died, somewhere in the early 1940s."

"Why didn't Josie and her husband buy back the mansion when they got married? They must have had plenty of money. They could have fixed it up and moved in. Or if they didn't want to live there, they could have rented it out instead of leaving it to rot."

"That surprises me, too. Josie is awfully proud of the Kettering family and their position in Placer Bar. Davis moved here right after the Civil War with nothing going for him but a good mind and a strong back. He'd fought on the side of the Confederacy and he wasn't willing to live under Yankee rule. He made a lucky strike in mining and bought up a lot of land. Then he started the bank. The Ketterings have other interests now, in mining and ranching and the lumber business, but they owe it all to old Davis, who founded the family fortunes. You'd think that Josie would have wanted to turn the house into a memorial to him."

Carla nodded. "She could have endowed it as a museum."

Sally gave her a speculative look. "You seem to have an unusually strong feeling for old houses."

Alarm bells went off in Carla's head. Did Sally realize that she'd become obsessed with the mansion? Had she somehow learned about Carla's unhappy marriage? Her mouth filled with the coppery taste of fear. "No," she gasped. "That's not true!"

Sally looked puzzled. "I just meant that I could lend you some books on the history of the area."

"Oh. Books." The rush of blood in her ears faded. Carla forced her breathing back under control. "That would be nice."

Sally stared at her for a moment, then decided to let it pass. She knelt in front of the bookshelf under the TV set. She rummaged around and finally decided on a couple of volumes, an old-looking book bound in blue leather and a new one with a burlap cover. "I make a hobby of local history," she said as she handed them over.

"Thanks." Carla had recovered from her scare, but she couldn't shake the feeling that she'd had a narrow escape. She glanced at her watch and jumped to her feet. "Whoops!" she cried with artificial gaiety. "I've got to hit the grocery store before Peter gets home."

She could tell that Sally didn't know what to make of her behavior, but she didn't care. She grabbed the books and fled out the door.

What had she been thinking of in going to visit Sally? Carla asked herself this question as she hurried down the street toward the supermarket. Where had she gotten the idea that she could make a new friend?

The last remains of her panic faded and the familiar depression seeped in to take its place. Sally was a nice enough person, but she, Carla, was in no condition to establish a normal relationship with anyone. She'd gone from being miserable to being seriously neurotic, and she didn't want to get close to anyone for fear they'd find out. Even the most casual sort of companionship was out of the question.

Sighing, she put the books in the basket of a supermarket shopping cart and wheeled it in through the store entrance.

Chapter 6

Roaming the aisles of the grocery had its usual calming effect on Carla's nerves. By the time she'd passed through the checkout line she felt thoroughly ashamed of the abrupt way she'd run out on Sally. She'd telephone her tomorrow, she resolved, and invite her over for a return cup of coffee. She owed her that much out of common politeness.

She carried her groceries home, put a pot roast on to boil, then decided to call Lieutenant Pressner at the police station to find out how the case was going. "Have you caught the killer yet?" she asked him when she was finally put through.

"He didn't leave his calling card under the body." Pressner sighed patiently, conveying that he was a busy man and he'd done her a big favor by accepting her call. "We had to bring in a forensic team from Sacramento, and it'll probably be a week or two before they report back to us. They tend to give our rural cases a low priority, and since this murder is twenty years old, they haven't classified it as a rush job. I doubt if they'll find anything, anyway. Fingerprints don't last forever, you know. They're nothing but a thin film of grease and they usually evaporate after a few years."

"What about the victim? Have you gotten a line on his identity?"

"No luck there, either. We're checking missing persons

records, but I'm not optimistic. Even that costume he was wearing was homemade. We didn't find any labels, even in his boots. Right now our main hope is that somebody will come in and identify the guy."

"I'd have thought you'd have gotten a few calls by now."

"We've had dozens." His sigh was even louder this time. "From what people tell us, back in the seventies this town was swarming with suspicious-looking men with long dark hair and dark goatees. Unfortunately, all of them were about six feet tall, the hulking, burly type."

"But shouldn't you be talking to people, asking questions? There may be witnesses out there who are reluctant to approach you for one reason or another."

"Ms. Weber, half the residents of this town had some contact with the hippies. We've got a few leads that we're following up, but we don't have the manpower to interview hundreds of people for practically no reason."

His voice grew even more patronizing. "We know what we're doing. You can leave this murder safely to us. Incidentally, we're through at the mansion, so you can go back whenever you're ready. I'd suggest that you forget about the dead man and get on with your interior decorating."

Carla felt far from satisfied as she hung up the phone. The more she brooded about it, the more terrible it seemed that a murder could have occurred at the house she loved. She wanted to see the killer caught and put behind bars. And if that was impossible, she wanted the victim identified, at the very least. It would exorcise some of the sheer wrongness of the situation if the poor man could be buried decently under his own name.

And it was all very well for Pressner to tell her to stay out of the case, but she didn't see how that would be possible. The victim's picture was screaming from every television set, splashed all over the front page of the local paper. She'd picked up a copy of the Placer Bar Herald at the grocery store and it was practically the only story they'd written about. The murder was sure to be a major topic of conversation in town. Her work on the history of the mansion would involve talking to people, asking them what they remembered of the house in the old days, and it was too much to expect that her informants would keep strictly to the nineteenth century. They were bound to want to talk about the hippies.

The thought heartened her. She clipped the police artist's sketch out of the newspaper, the picture showing how the dead man must have looked when he was still alive, and folded it carefully into her wallet for future reference.

Carla was still feeling a little spooked by her discovery of the body the next morning, so she decided to start her day with a little paperwork at City Hall. Placer Bar was sure to have records on the mansion; maybe she could get the names of some of the hippies who'd lived there.

City Hall was an ancient structure on Broad Street that had been given an Art Deco facade by the Works Project Administration back in the Depression. It wasn't a large building, but the corridors twisted in a confusing manner. Carla wandered the halls until she saw a door labeled "Planning Department." A middle-aged woman sat behind a counter reading a paperback romance novel.

She grew visibly excited when Carla asked for the file on the Kettering mansion. "I heard about the murder. Are you a reporter, doing a story on the house? Weird old place. Must hold a lot of ghosts. The tales those walls could tell!"

Her face fell when Carla made it clear that she was after facts, not colorful rumors, but she produced a manila folder from the row of filing cabinets banked behind her. The file was surprisingly slim considering the age and importance of the house. All it contained was a photocopy of a 1942 Trust Deed transferring the property from Howard Kettering to a Mr. And Mrs. Edwin Wilson, the couple that had run the boarding house; a notice that the town had seized the property for back taxes in 1965; and a condemnation order dated January, 1978. The top paper in the file was the deed giving title to the Stauffers. Carla was interested to see that they'd only paid $60,000—although, of course, that was well beyond anything she could afford, and it would cost many times that amount to make the house habitable.

Carla handed the file back. "Actually, Mrs. Williams—" she read the woman's name off a plaque on the counter. "I was hoping you might have records dating back a little further. The architect's original blueprints, something like that." She spread her hands to acknowledge that she appreciated the audacity of her request. She knew from past experience that clerks hated to search out old records. They were invariably kept in cardboard boxes in a musty storeroom overrun with spiders.

"You do want to go back a ways. Almost all our records from that period have been destroyed." The woman gave her a sociable smile. "If we ever even had any documents like that, they probably would have been destroyed during the fire of 1894 when the first City Hall burned down. Or then again, they could have been lost in the chaos during World War II. Things got pretty bad towards the end there."

Carla didn't know what to make of this last statement. "World War II? What chaos? Surely Placer Bar wasn't invaded."

Mrs. Williams shook her head. "The Gray Ladies. The lady volunteers who knitted things for the soldiers."

"The Gray Ladies attacked City Hall?"

Mrs. Williams was losing her patience. "There was a whole lot going on back then. They had to fit in the Red Cross, the Gray Ladies, the Civil Defense people—space was tight. They tossed out a lot of the old papers to make room." She sounded sorry not to have been there to help with the tossing.

"Oh." Carla could see she'd put the woman's back up. She cast about in her mind for a way to shift the conversation to the 1970's and decided on the direct approach. She took the artist's re-creation of the dead man out of her purse. "I don't suppose you had many dealings with the hippies that moved into house after it was abandoned?"

Mrs. Williams visibly defrosted as her eyes fell on the newspaper clipping. "That's the man who was murdered, isn't it? Not that I'd recognize the fellow. Those hippies! They didn't want to have anything to do with the authorities, I can tell you that. Of course, they couldn't go their own way entirely. There was a young girl who used to come in here when they had problems with the city. She called herself Moonfern, I believe. An awfully cute little things." She chuckled reminiscently. "She had the building inspector twisted around her little finger. She even talked the utilities into reconnecting the water and electricity."

"You wouldn't remember her real name, would you?" Mrs. Williams shook her head. "What about the building inspector? Would he know?"

"Mr. Upfield passed away three years ago."

"The water company! She must have paid the water bills by check."

"That she did, but her bank account was in the name of Moonfern, too. A friend of mine worked for the billing department and she thought it was a riot. It's legal, you know. You can call yourself anything you want to here in California, so long as there's no intent to defraud."

These officials had been much too easy-going, Carla thought irritably. Why couldn't they have asked for formal identification before opening an account? Moonfern was probably a successful lawyer these days, operating under a name like Kimberly Armstrong-Bates. She'd be impossible to trace.

"Then there was her boyfriend. What was his name—Long Bow? Straight Arrow? Something like that."

"Didn't you know any of them by their real names?" Carla begged.

Mrs. Williams seemed vaguely put out by the question. "Well, I'm not sure about the boyfriend. Maybe he was a Native American or something."

This did not seem like a promising lead. Carla was beginning to appreciate the magnitude of the task Lieutenant Pressner was facing. Discouraged, she turned away.

"You might try the Assessor's Office," Mrs. Williams called after her. They were friends again now that Carla was taking her unreasonable requests for information elsewhere. "He has plot maps dating back to 1869. He keeps all the old records they saved from the City Hall fire." She gave Carla directions to a room down the hall.

The clerk in the Assessor's Office was about the same age as Mrs. Williams, but where she'd been vague to the point of carelessness, he was the obsessive type. Mr. Logan firmly denied having had anything to do with the hippies, although he remembered them well. "They occupied the building illegally, and since they didn't pay taxes, they didn't come under my jurisdiction," he insisted. He ran a hand nervously through his thinning gray hair as Carla explained her research project, and when she asked to see his plot maps he reacted with suspicion, as if she were asking to see a top secret government file and he wasn't at all sure that she had the proper security clearance.

He finally unbent enough to allow her access to the public records. Sure enough, the Kettering mansion was shown on several surveys. The most detailed information came from the 1869 plot map, a sort of primitive aerial photograph hand-drawn on a huge sheet of heavy paper. Not only did the map show the town lots, the actual 1869 buildings were marked out with dotted lines.

The Kettering mansion was over at the far edge of the map, but the surveyor hadn't skimped on his work. In addition to the house, the drawing showed a number of outbuildings which had disappeared by now. The structures weren't labeled, but Carla tentatively identified a stables, an outdoor kitchen and a summer house at the end of the garden. She hadn't learned much about the hippies, but she was making progress on the work she was doing for Bronwin, she reflected as she held the relevant part of the big sheet of paper over the Assessor's copy machine.

This seemed to have exhausted the resources of City Hall. She tucked the copy in her briefcase and decided that her next step was to approach Josie Kettering. Josie might remember how the mansion had looked when Davis Kettering lived there, before the rooms were chopped up and it was converted into a boarding house. What was more, she might well have been sufficiently shocked when the hippies moved in to take a jealous interest in their carryings-on.

Carla stopped at a pay phone in the City Hall lobby and called Josie to explain what she wanted, taking care to emphasize that the restoration project would redound to the credit of the Kettering name.

"I don't have time to see you today," Josie interrupted before she could finish. "Anyway, it wouldn't be worth your while to come over. I wouldn't be able to help."

"I'm sure you know more about the house than you realize."

Josie snorted, but Carla refused to be discouraged. "If today is bad, could I drop by tomorrow? I really need to talk to you. It's part of my job."

"Oh, all right. I suppose if you're determined, you might as well come now. But I warn you, you'll be wasting your time."

Carla hurried over to Josie's house, anxious to get there before the banker's wife changed her mind. Josie seemed upset when she opened the door.

"This dreadful murder!" she burst out. "You'd think that Bronwin would give up on the house now that they've found a dead body hidden in the wall. It's morbid, that's what it is. You might as well fix up a crypt and move in and set up housekeeping."

Carla was taken aback by the image. "I guess Bronwin doesn't see it that way," she murmured. "After all, most old houses have had people die in them."

"Of course, but murder's very different. And very few old houses have been used as mausoleums!"

Josie was in terrific form today. Carla decided it would be useless to argue. "The hippies must have seemed strange to you," she said as she followed the older woman into the living room. "Did you ever meet any of them?"

Josie was so surprised by this question that she didn't even take offense. "Certainly not," she said in a wondering tone. "They were scarcely the sort of people I'd want to spend my time with.

"I felt sorry for them," she went on, sitting down on the beige love seat and waving Carla to a chair. "They were out of touch with reality. They weren't like you and me, hardworking people who give our lives meaning by doing the best we can for our families. Those hippies, they lived for the day. They talked about peace and love and freedom, but all it came down to was, they didn't really care about anybody else and nobody cared for them."

Carla was surprised by this analysis. It was hard to think of Josie as an altruistic person. Still, she had a point. Carla suspected she'd be happier if she spent less time thinking about her own problems and more time worrying about Peter.

"Take that corpse the cops are trying to identify," Josie went on. "Normally when a man disappears, his relatives ask questions. They try to discover what happened to him. But in this case, nobody bothered. The police can't find a missing persons report, and nobody has come forward to identify the body. I'll bet the man was a runaway, estranged from his family, and his friends wouldn't have thought twice about it when he dropped out of sight. We may never find out what his name was, or where he came from."

It was a depressing thought. Carla sighed. "I know you're busy and I won't keep you. I just thought you might have some old photographs of the Kettering mansion. What I'd really like would be architectural drawings showing the house the way it was first built."

"I wouldn't have anything like that. It's silly to keep records after they've outlived their usefulness. The Ketterings have been active in business for well over a century, and if we'd saved all our old papers—why, they'd crowd us out of house and home." The idea must have been a gratifying one, for Josie's expression relaxed a little. "I might have a few old photos, though. I think my husband keeps an album in his den."

She led Carla to a room that looked more like a magazine illustration than a working office. Matching red leather chairs, the upholstery attached by rows of shining brass studs, faced a broad, low fieldstone fireplace. A Persian rug of impressive size and quality glowed on the floor. Glass-fronted bookcases held sets of leatherbound classics and a roll-top desk stood open in one corner, its pigeonholes stuffed artfully with yellowed maps and deeds. The writing surface was bare except for a stand holding a crystal inkwell and a matching sand caster, and a Chinese jar holding a collection of nibbed pens.

To Carla's surprise, the drawers of the desk were jammed full with working stationery and the usual worthless clutter that desks tend to accumulate. Packs of worn playing cards were jumbled in together with loose rubber bands and paper clips and stray ballpoint pens. The top drawer on the right held an astonishing number of the leatherette-covered pocket notebooks that businesses tend to give away as a promotion during the Christmas holidays.

Josie rummaged carelessly through this mess, disturbing it still further, until she unearthed a small clothbound photograph album, just large enough to hold one picture per page. She sat down in the swivel desk chair and opened it on the desk.

"Howard's father, Roger, put this album together." Josie lowered her eyes to express conventional sorrow and Carla gathered that Roger had died. "He had a wonderful feeling for family history. I'm sure he would have been able to help with your questions."

Josie flipped through the book and Carla, bending over her shoulder, watched with interest as old sepia-tinted photographs of Placer Bar and its residents slipped through Josie's fingers. Carla reached out a hand to stop her as the picture of a pretty young woman in the dress of the late Victorian period came into view. "Who was that?"

"Let me see—that might have been Davis's wife, Bessie. She was quite a bit younger than he was. No, Bessie had bigger ears. It must be one of her sisters, or a cousin." Josie turned a page. "Here's Davis himself."

A worn-looking elderly man stood next to a 1920's touring car on the gravel drive leading to the mansion. He leaned forward on a long umbrella, his hands folded over its handle. He was staring at the camera suspiciously, or perhaps his eyes were simply narrowed against the sun. A small section of the left-hand corner of the house could be seen in the background.

"Can I borrow that?" Carla asked. "I'd like to have a copy made. It might help with the restoration work." The picture didn't really contain any useful information, but she thought it would be a nice addition to the file she was assembling on the house. It would be something Bronwin could show people when she told them about her restoration project.

A few minutes earlier, Josie had dismissed old records as being of no importance. Now she looked doubtful. "I'd hate to break up the book."

"No problem. The pictures aren't glued in." Carla plucked the photograph from its old-fashioned cardboard corner holders.

"Well—be sure and return it when you're through."

They went through the book and managed to isolate a dozen pictures showing the house. The album was arranged in rough chronological order and towards the end, there were a number of snapshots of a young man. Josie identified him as Howard, her husband. These weren't records of Howard's leisure moments; they were trophy photos taken to celebrate business deals. Judging from the cut of the men's suits, the pictures had been taken in the late 1950's or early 1960's. Howard was invariably shown standing with a group of other men, all of them gazing over fields or staring down mine shafts with a proprietary air. Carla wondered who the photographer had been who accompanied Howard Kettering on these excursions.

Josie replaced the album in the desk drawer and leaned back in the elaborately carved swivel chair. "The mansion must have been lovely when Davis was still alive," Carla encouraged her. "What I'm trying to find out is what it looked like inside. What colors were the walls painted, or were they covered with wallpaper? Can you tell me about the window treatments? It would really help if you could remember specific pieces of furniture, and how they were arranged."

"I wouldn't have a clue. I never even set foot in the house until well after Howard and I got married. That was in 1952, and his parents had sold the mansion to the boarding house couple ten years earlier, right after Davis died. Howard's parents had their own house, of course, a modern one, and there was no reason for them to hang onto the old place. So when I first saw the interior, the mansion had been functioning as a sort of cheap hotel for long-term guests for several years, and it was not what you'd describe as elegant. I could tell you about the naugahyde chairs and the black-and-white TV in the lounge, if you'd like. Howard and I stopped by the place for some reason, and what I mainly remember is the cheap paint the new owners had slapped over the new partitions they'd put up to make extra rooms."

Carla shook her head sympathetically. "When was the house built?"

"Sometime in the 1870's, I'd imagine. I could ask Howard, but I doubt if he'd know the precise date." Josie pursed her lips. "It was a silly thing to do, really, building a Southern mansion in the Sierra foothills. Those houses were designed to stay cool in the hot Carolina summers, not to withstand a mountain snowstorm. But I suppose Davis longed for something to remind him of home. He moved to Placer Bar after the Civil War ended. He'd fought with the Confederate forces and he was the only one in his family to make it through the war alive. He came out West to make a fresh start after the Yankees confiscated their lands."

Josie's voice was gaining in volume. She was bragging again. Carla figured her best bet was to play up to her. "I understand that Davis was extremely successful here."

"He was a brilliant businessman. Davis got his start in mining—made a lucky find. He used that money to buy land in the Central Valley, good farming acreage. If someone came to him with an interesting business idea, he'd invest, and of course he'd pocket his share of the profits. He established the bank before the turn of the century."

"The Kettering mansion has been remodeled a number of times. Did Davis make any of the changes?"

"He put in the plumbing and wiring, I suppose. I know he had electric lights. But even with the improvements, the house is impossible. It's so old-fashioned—unsafe, really. They ought to tear the place down before somebody gets hurt."

Josie spoke with tremendous heat. Carla was baffled by her attitude. Why was she so passionate in her disapproval of the house? People who'd grown up without modern conveniences, who'd trudged to outhouses in the dead of winter and suffered through heat waves without the benefit of air conditioning, who'd had to haul heavy buckets of water from a creek to eat or drink or bathe, sometimes looked on old houses with vivid dislike. But Josie seemed a bit young for this, unless she'd been raised on some out-of-the-way farm.

"The mansion is an antique," Carla offered tactfully. "That's its charm."

Josie pushed back the swivel chair and stood up abruptly. "Bronwin Stauffer is just trying to make people pay attention to her. That's what this crazy restoration project is all about. If you'll take my advice, you'll steer clear of the whole mess."

How resentful she was, Carla told herself. Maybe she felt that the Stauffers were making her look bad by taking care of a job she should have done herself, restoring the Kettering family home.

"I've committed myself to the job. I can't back out now." Carla tucked the photographs in her briefcase before the older woman could change her mind. "I must be going. I've taken up enough of your time."

"Yes." Josie's voice grew mild. She seemed deflated, even a little embarrassed by her earlier vehemence. "Well, keep in touch. Let me know how you're getting along with the project."

She had a wistful, slightly baffled look on her face as she showed Carla to the door.

Chapter 7

Carla had almost reached home when she caught sight of a familiar mane of long black hair bobbing up the street ahead of her. "Sally, wait up!" she called. Sally was a local woman in her early forties, just the right age, she told herself as she sprinted to catch up with her. If anybody could tell her about the hippies, Sally could.

"Can I buy you a cup of coffee?" she panted as she drew level with her friend.

"I'd love to talk, but I don't have time right now. I'm on my way to a ceramics class."

"I'll walk along with you, then. Say, did you read in the paper about the dead body they found out at the old Kettering place?"

Sally gave her a quick glance. "Didn't somebody tell me that Bronwin hired you to help with the restoration work?"

Carla nodded vigorously. "I'm supposed to be looking into the history of the house, finding out how it was decorated when it was first built. But the murder is a more modern mystery, and now I'm interested in the hippie period. Did you ever meet any of those people?"

Sally's eyes softened and her lips curved in a reminiscent smile. "I spent a lot of time at the old Kettering house the summer after I graduated from high school, soon after the hippies discovered the mansion and moved in. They were an interesting bunch, just enough older than I was to make me think they were terribly sophisticated. Do you remember how impressive people in their twenties were when you were seventeen?"

Carla made an encouraging noise and lengthened her stride to match Sally's.

"They threw parties every weekend, with live music. Sometimes they'd have three or four bands, amateur groups but good ones, playing in different rooms. The food was always terrible, though. The women would bake incredibly dense loaves of homemade bread. You'd have to rip a bite off with your teeth and chew it for ten minutes before you could swallow. They were forever experimenting with vegetarian food, and they'd use so many spices that a simple dish of carrots would be inedible. Anything to be different." She giggled. "I remember once they dug a pit and roasted a whole pig. What a disaster! When they scraped the coals off, the animal's fat had turned green!"

"So you hung around on the fringes of the group?"

"I had a huge crush on one of the boys. What was his name—Bill? Bob? Something like that. He was into meditation, and he was always busy with his yoga when I wanted him to pay attention to me. He didn't take our romance very seriously, but my parents sure did. They were relieved when fall came and it was time for me to leave for U.C. Davis."

Pressner was right. Nobody remembered the hippies very well after all this time. "What happened next?" Carla asked.

"I started going out with Charles, my husband. After that, I didn't have any time for the people at the Kettering place."

"Do you have any theories about the murder?" They'd reached the Arts Center, an overgrown wooden cottage where classes were held. Carla leaned against the porch railing.

Sally's expression grew serious. "Knowing that gang, I'd

say it was probably motivated by sex. Some redneck father shot the man who'd seduced his daughter and refused to make an honest woman out of her. Or jealousy might have been the motive. I know that several women in town had affairs with guys who lived out there." She grimaced. "Men, too. Half the married men in town were fascinated by the idea of getting it on with a hippie chick. The more conservative they were in their everyday lives, the more the thought seemed to appeal to them."

"What about drugs?" Carla prompted.

"Could have been. Most of the hippies were decent sorts and they tried to keep it clean, but every so often they'd get a hard case. I remember one day I walked in on a man shooting up in the kitchen. He'd tied his arm off and he was melting heroine in a spoon. Heroine has always been a gun drug. The dealers and a lot of the users pack weapons."

Carla felt a moment's revulsion. Had her corpse been a dealer who'd been killed by one of his customers? Or a junkie who'd stolen from the wrong person to pay for his habit? No! He'd been an innocent victim, she told herself, someone like Sally. He'd wandered onto the scene looking for good music and bad food, and had accidentally gotten in the way of something serious that was happening.

Sally glanced at her watch. Her class was starting, she said. The two of them parted, exchanging promises to get together soon. Who should she talk to next? Carla asked herself as she walked away. Well, there was Maud Rucker. She probably wouldn't know much about the hippies, having been the wrong generation to make friends with them, but she might be able to tell her about the house. Josie had said Maud was a member of a long-standing local family, and she could well have been a regular visitor back in the old days.

Carla remembered the sandwiches Maud had helped herself to at the party and she decided it might be a good idea to arrive with food in hand. She stopped by her house and filled a paper grocery sack with foil-wrapped trout from the refrigerator freezer. She'd finally have room to store a few groceries besides fish. She retraced her way up Broad Street to the decaying Victorian Sally had pointed out.

Steve Rucker answered the door. He obviously remembered her from their run-in on the banks of the creek, and he seemed disconcerted to encounter her on his home territory. He glanced at her, startled, then turned his eyes away. He backed into the hall, giving her room to enter, and bolted out the door, muttering something about an appointment.

"He's shy with strangers."

Carla turned to find Maud standing behind her. The elderly woman grinned, showing long yellow teeth.

"I've brought you some trout," Carla said, handing her the heavy sack.

"Aren't you sweet." Maud peered into the bag with pleasure, counting under her breath, evidently estimating the number of meals it contained. She headed for the back of the house at a slow hobble and Carla followed, glowing with the satisfaction of having disposed of her excess food by giving it to someone who would really use it.

Maud's kitchen hadn't been remodeled in fifty years and this was a case where a few improvements would have been in order. The stove was cast iron. The stained porcelain sink was set in a homemade counter topped with linoleum that matched the threadbare linoleum on the floor, and there weren't any cabinets, only a freestanding hutch of painted wood. Maud put the trout in an ancient refrigerator, the kind with a motor in a circular housing on top, and led the way back to the front room.

The main body of the house was about what Carla had

expected, a once respectable residence that had fallen on evil days. The walls had faded to dirty shades of pink and green and beige, and water spots marred the ceilings. The parlor was swept and dusted, though, and Maud kept it well-aired. The room didn't have a musty smell like so many old houses did.

Maud sat on a corner of the sofa on a spot where the brocade was especially worn. Carla took a rump-sprung chair and explained her errand.

"I haven't been to the Kettering mansion in years," the older woman said musingly. "I never had occasion to visit the boarding house, and lately, of course, it's been boarded up. I spent a lot of time there as a young girl, though. My mother and Bessie Kettering were good friends."

"Pay dirt!" thought Carla.

"There was a window seat in the front room," Maud went on. "How I loved that window seat—I'd like to see it replaced if it's gone now. It had green velvet cushions that matched the velvet drapes. I felt like a princess, sitting there looking out over the garden."

Her eyes changed focus, as if she were staring into the past. "The living room had beautiful wallpaper, great bunches of purple violets. When I was a girl, I thought it was the last word in elegance. And the front hallway was yellow, I think. I remember yellow sunlight on yellow walls when we entered the house."

Then she sighed and her voice regained its matter-of-fact tone. "I'm afraid this isn't much help."

It had been long ago, and it wasn't surprising Maud's memories were patchy. "I talked to Josie Kettering before I came here," Carla said. "She didn't have much to tell me. I think she could have been more cooperative if she'd wanted to, but she's still opposed to the restoration project. She seems to hate the house, and she must have a reason to feel so strongly. Did Davis Kettering do something terrible to her when she was young?

Maud seemed surprised by the idea. "Not that I've heard. Josie grew up here in Placer Bar, but she was just a kid when Davis died. I don't know if he was even aware of her existence. Maybe he would have opposed her marriage to Howard if he'd still been alive when it happened, but of course he wasn't. Josie and Howard's engagement caused a lot of talk around town. Josie's parents weren't entirely respectable."

Maud went on talking, relishing the long-ago mini-scandal. "You have to understand that family background was awfully important back in those days. People were much more class conscious than they are now. Today almost anyone can get an education, and even travel if they want to, but at that time there was a much bigger gap between rich and poor.

"Josie and Howard were a genuine love match," she continued. "Josie's a few years younger than he is, so they didn't know each other very well. Then Josie took a job as a teller at the bank. Two weeks later, they announced they were getting married. Roger and Mabel, Howard's parents, weren't too happy about it, but Howard refused to listen to them. He can be pretty stubborn when something's important to him. I took the side of the young couple. I've always admired Josie for her pluck. She's an energetic little thing."

Carla looked at Maud in surprise. It was difficult for her to imagine the well-padded middle-aged matron as a dashing young girl. What was more, Maud seemed to feel protective toward Josie. She wondered why, especially after the dirty trick Josie had pulled with the raw liver.

Of course, it sounded as if the two women went back a long way. They probably had a fairly complex relationship. She decided not to question Maud's assessment of Josie's character.

"I guess it's just Bronwin who's got Josie so upset, then."

"I think you're right." Maud hesitated a moment, weighing her words, then went on with her story. "Josie's father abandoned his family when she was twelve, and her mother's reputation was—unsavory, shall we say. Josie spent her early years trying to live down the malicious gossip, so social position is very important to her. She thinks of herself as a Kettering now, a rich and respectable pillar of the community. It's not surprising if she resents Bronwin's trying to horn in on the Kettering name. And now that the cops have found that dead body—well, the whole thing just doesn't look good. Josie probably feels that it reflects badly on her."

Carla produced the artist's reconstruction of the dead man's face from her wallet. "The cops are still trying to make an identification. You don't recognize him, do you?"

Maud peered at the clipping and smiled. "Looks like a generic hippie to me." Carla had to admit that the drawing was a little lacking in character.

She asked a few more questions about the mansion, but Maud didn't have much to add. She'd never been upstairs, she said. Davis and his wife Bessie had entertained formally, with servants, and their guests rarely strayed from the front reception salons.

Maud suggested that Carla visit the Placer County Historical Society. She told her where to find it, a few blocks away.

Carla spent the rest of the day in the small brick building that housed the library-museum. She rummaged through their file of old pictures and was delighted when she came across a lithograph of the Kettering mansion in an old county history. The house was painted a pale color, probably white, with a dark front door. A horse-drawn carriage waited on the drive and a group of people in formal dress lingered in the foreground, presumably to show that the house had been a magnet for Placer Bar's fashionable set in the late nineteenth century. Carla made a copy of the drawing, reflecting as she did so that she was assembling an interesting collection of documents.

It was too bad that she hadn't discovered any leads to the identity of the murdered man. The thought continued to worry her. She knew she was being unreasonable, but she couldn't help feeling that the house was counting on her for an answer. She'd let it down badly.

Carla had always felt that buildings possessed personalities of their own, complete with faint, slow-moving emotions. Some houses seemed to enjoy being lived in; they responded to and returned the affection their inhabitants felt for their welcoming shelter. Others were indifferent or even hostile. She'd had a strong sense of connection with the Kettering mansion from the very beginning. She'd sensed that the house appreciated her visits, that it greeted her with pleasure.

Her discovery of the body had changed their relationship. The house had entrusted her with its secret and implored her help. She'd incurred an obligation and until she'd discharged it, she was afraid the house would reproach her, even reject her as a friend. Whatever happened, she wouldn't be at peace with the house until she'd discovered the identity of the man in the military jacket.

Chapter 8

Carla caught the TV news that night and listened to the radio the next morning. The cops hadn't made any progress in identifying the body.

She snapped off the radio with a sense of frustration and poured yet another cup of breakfast coffee. She had to admit that she was reluctant to go back to the Kettering mansion. The memory of her last visit, with her violent irrational longing to possess the house, followed by the finding of a very real mummified body, made her skin itch. Plus she couldn't shake the feeling that the house was angry with her, disappointed that she couldn't put a name to the corpse. But, of course, she had a job to do. The contractor would show up in a few days and she had to be ready for him. She swallowed the last of the coffee and packed herself a picnic lunch, resolving to spend the day doing the work she'd been hired for.

Her shoulders tensed defensively as she let herself into the house, but the reproachful vibrations weren't too strong. She forced herself to ignore them and concentrate on finishing her rough floor plan.

The rooms on the first two floors were large and graciously proportioned if you ignored the flimsy partitions dividing them into smaller quarters, but the third floor was different. Here the rooms were small and oddly shaped, with slanted ceilings broken by dormer windows. These would have been servants' quarters and storerooms in the old days.

She found the trap door in the ceiling in a corner of one of the smaller rooms. A short rope dangled from the edge of the ceiling opening, ending just within her reach. She grabbed the frayed cord and gave it a tug. The trap door swung open and a folding staircase reeled slowly downward, stopping with a creak at head height. She grabbed the lowest step and pulled down the final section of the staircase until it rested securely on the floor. Black dirt, as greasy as the fine ash from a fireplace, leaped up to coat her hands.

She bounced a couple of times on the bottom step to make sure the wood was still sound enough to hold her weight, then mounted the steps. When she neared the top, she flicked on her flashlight. She was a little nervous about exploring the attic after her experience with the linen closet, but she told herself not to be foolish. She was hardly likely to find a second dead body up there.

The attic was smaller than the lower stories and only part of it was floored. The rest of the space was nothing but beams supporting the lath and plaster of the ceiling below. Carla played the beam of her flashlight around the large open room and the light bounced off a dark mass on the far edge of the floored area. Cardboard boxes! She scrambled the rest of the way up the stairs into the attic.

The boxes were a disappointment at first. She pawed through a collection of uninteresting old clothes and a hoard of canceled checks dating from the 1950's. No wonder the owners had left these things behind. Then she opened the final box. This was more like it—she'd found a wealth of 78 rpm phonograph records, many of them Beethoven symphonies.

She decided to take the records downstairs. She supposed

she'd have to hand them over to the Stauffers, but if they didn't want them, she'd keep them for herself.

She'd almost finished tugging the heavy box to the head of the staircase when her flashlight picked up a shadow on the plaster and lath of the unfinished part of the attic. She waved the light in a circle and elicited a faint gleam from the darkness. Abandoning the records, she went to investigate.

Whatever the object was, it was a good way out from the floored area. She picked a path from beam to beam, careful not to put a foot through the plaster ceiling of the room below, until she reached the spot and could hunker down in a stable crouch. Lying in the dust was a small folding pocket ruler, made of wood and hinged and bound with brass.

She opened it up. The foot rule was divided into four three-inch sections, arranged to fold into a narrow packet. A delicate brass caliper rule set into the last piece added a further three inches when she pulled it out. The caliper rule was marked in one-thirty-seconds of an inch calibrations for fine measuring jobs, while the hinged wooden pieces had the usual one-six-teenth inch markings.

Carla was delighted with her find. This was just the sort of thing she'd always wanted to discover in an attic. She put the ruler in her pocket and made her way back to the floored area.

The record albums were heavy and it took her several trips to carry them down from the attic to the front hall. By the time she'd finished, she was ready for an early lunch.

Moving the records had been a filthy job. Carla was covered with more than a century's accumulation of fine black attic grime. She beat the worst of it out of her clothes, then washed her face and arms at the kitchen sink. When she was reasonably clean, she took her sandwiches out to the back porch steps.

It was a relief to be outside, away from the house's faint

reproachful presence. Here in the sunlight, with the air charged with fragrance from a bush of old roses that bordered the back steps, she could forget about the dead man and enjoy her peanut butter sandwich.

She lingered over the thermos of orange juice, then went back in the house. The next step was to see if she could find traces of the original wallpapers.

The work was exacting and she soon became absorbed. She was steaming the walls of a little alcove under the stairs, a refuge furnished with a built-in bench where visiting ladies could sit down and take off their overshoes, when the rattle of the front door broke into her concentration.

Alarmed again, but this time by the thought of intruders, she put down the wet newspapers and the hairdryer she was using for the steaming job and went to investigate. Bronwin Stauffer was standing in the hall, peering up the staircase with an inquiring look on her face.

Damnation! This was the last thing she needed on a difficult day, Carla told herself ruefully. If the house was going to make her feel uncomfortable, why couldn't it pull its tricks on Bronwin?

"There you are," Bronwin said. "I thought I'd drop by and make sure you hadn't unearthed any more dead bodies."

"I haven't made a whole lot of progress yet," Carla admitted. She rubbed her nose with a finger. Her hands were dirty again, and she realized she'd probably left a black smudge on her face. She dusted her hands off and made an effort to swallow her irritation. Bronwin was her employer, she reminded herself. If she was going to take the woman's paycheck, she owed it to her to be polite.

She started to tell Bronwin about her efforts to recreate the original floor plan, but her employer interrupted with a frown.

"Hey, I'm not planning to move a lot of walls around. I'm not that compulsive about historical accuracy. I just want the rooms to look the way they did when Davis Kettering first built the house. It'll be fun to be able to say that I've restored the original color scheme."

Carla shrugged. "If paint and wallpaper are all you care about, that'll make my job a lot easier."

Bronwin brushed past her into the front parlor. "What color was this room, for instance?"

"We're going to *have* to do some construction work in here," Carla protested. She gestured to the right. "See that wall? It's nothing more than cheap wallboard, and they tore out some of the plaster frieze on the ceiling when they put it up. We really ought to take it out, and then we'll need to make molds and cast new sections to replace the plaster they destroyed."

Bronwin gazed at the partition. "I suppose that would give me a nice big room for entertaining."

Carla nodded stiffly. Bronwin's lack of feeling for the house was a source of constant annoyance. "As to how this room was decorated, I'm not sure I can help you."

She glanced around. A gas heater had been installed in the fireplace, but the original mantel was still there. She walked over and chipped loose a shallow section of paint at the corner where the mantel met the wall, using a chisel to cut into the plaster. The remains of old paint and wallpaper were most likely to be found in hard-to-reach spots like this one where they would be hard to scrape away.

Carla examined the thin chip of plaster carefully. No traces of wallpaper remained. There was just a layer of institutional green under the grubby white surface paint.

"I suppose this room was green, then." Bronwin sounded disappointed; it was an ugly color.

"I don't think so. They generally used wallpaper in formal reception areas back when this house was built. The trouble is, this room has probably been redecorated more than once. In a bedroom, people might save themselves trouble by painting over the wallpaper. But in an important room like this one, they usually do a thorough job, stripping the walls before they paint. I'm afraid the original wall coverings are long gone."

"I think it's a crime the way the Ketterings let this place deteriorate," Bronwin fumed.

"In a way, you're lucky that they didn't bother to keep the house up. People often do a lot of damage when they modernize. At least the original hardware is still intact." Carla pointed out the fine brass doorknob and key plate, engraved with a design of geometrical leaves and flowers, on the parlor door. "And you're lucky that people haven't broken in and stolen things—collectors or antique dealers or even kids. They don't just take the hardware. I've seen cases where they've used crowbars to tear away the fireplace tiles and the wainscoting off the walls."

Bronwin looked suitabiy impressed.

"I found some stuff in the attic," Carla went on. "Look at these old 78s." She pointed to the stack of record albums she'd piled near the front door. "I guess they belong to you, now."

Bronwin was less than thrilled. "I don't think they'd play very well on my cd changer," she sniffed.

Carla didn't know whether to be irritated by Bronwin's attitude or happy that she could keep the records for herself. She had an old stereo that would play them just fine. Before she could respond, Bronwin started for the door. "Well, I'll leave you to it. I'm late for the Arts Center Board Meeting."

"I didn't know you belonged."

"Owen and I joined as soon as we decided to move to Placer Bar. We're big on public service. They're having an election next week. I'm running for President, and that means I have to go to their stupid meetings."

Carla's jaw dropped at this fresh evidence of the woman's lack of sensitivity, but then she noticed that Bronwin was watching to catch her reaction. Bronwin was playing a joke. Evidently she hadn't been as successful at hiding her dislike of her boss as she'd supposed.

She laughed to hide her embarrassment. "I suppose we all have our crosses to bear."

Carla followed Bronwin to the front door and watched her stride down the overgrown drive to her car. She idly wondered why Bronwin had decided to run for the presidency of the Arts Center. Did she think it would help her become accepted in Placer Bar—or did she just like the idea of defeating someone who really wanted the job? Carla didn't believe for one moment that Bronwin was interested in helping the local artists. She shook her head in amusement. She'd be curious to see if Bronwin won.

Then she realized that she'd forgotten to mention the folding pocket ruler. Oh, well, surely it didn't matter. If Bronwin didn't care about Beethoven symphonies, she wouldn't want an old foot rule. It wasn't as if the thing had any value.

Still shaking her head, Carla turned and went back in the house.

Chapter 9

Carla spent the next couple of days scraping and chipping at the mansion's walls. By Friday, she'd identified six wallpaper patterns she was convinced were originals, but she knew there must have been others of which no traces remained. Bronwin would just have to use her imagination and a guide to period wallpapers when it came time to decorate some of the rooms.

Lieutenant Pressner still hadn't discovered the identity of the dead man. The house seemed resigned to this, but Carla sensed that the mansion was in a surly mood. It had asked her to scrub out the old bloodstains, not to cover them with wallpaper and paint.

Adding to her problems, the contractor was scheduled to begin work next week. Carla had mixed feelings about this. On the one hand, she hated the thought of intruders, who would disturb her peaceful possession of the house. On the other, she had to admit that the workmen would keep her grounded. She wouldn't be able to delude herself into thinking the house was hers, not with a gang of carpenters doing their earsplitting work with power tools in the next room.

The contractor showed up before she expected. She was musing over a scrap of wallpaper in the front hall. It was yellow, as Maud remembered, but too small for her to make out a pattern. "Hello?" Someone rapped on the front door. A tall, wiry man with short-cropped brownish blond hair walked in without waiting for an answer. He was about her age and he fairly bristled with energy.

"Oh," he said, catching sight of her. "You must be Carla Weber. I'm sorry if I startled you. I'm Ned Fielding. We start work next week and I thought I'd come by and take a look at the job."

Her first reaction was resentment—what was he doing here? He wasn't supposed to visit the house until Monday. But she couldn't very well ask him to leave. "Come with me," she forced herself to offer. "I'll show you what we're up against."

Oblivious to her prickly attitude, he told her all about himself as she played the tour guide. He was a local resident, born and bred, married with two children, and his wife held a part-time job selling cosmetics door-to-door. They were renters at the moment, but they hoped to save enough money to build a house.

She warmed to him a little by the time they reached the attic. Ned was young enough to be flexible, but old enough to know what he was doing, Carla decided. He seemed to appreciate the difficulties he'd be facing, and he was very grateful for the work the old house would provide for his crew. "Times are rough," he told her. "If Owen hadn't hired me, I would have had to lay off some of my men."

He promised to help her in the search for the original floor plan. "Tell you what," he said. "I've got a young apprentice, Rob Lawry. He doesn't have a whole lot of experience, you understand, but he knows how to follow orders. I could lend him to you for a day or two if you want to look for old nail holes."

Carla smiled, won over by the offer. "This project could help you professionally. When we're through, you'll be able to tell people you've had experience with restoration work as well as new construction."

He gave her a cheerful grin. "Owen Stauffer's the man I'm anxious to impress at the moment. My wife and I will be able to swing our new house with no problem if he hires me to work on that new factory he's planning to build."

Bronwin had given Ned a set of keys, and since he wanted to poke around for a while longer, Carla left him to lock up. She was in a good mood as she walked down the drive toward home. She'd been lucky in Bronwin's choice of a contractor.

Then she noticed a large Ford pickup parked beyond the stone pillars. This was obviously Ned's work truck. She drew in her breath as she read the bumper stickers: "Don't Mess With This Truck If You Value Your Life", "This Car Protected By .357 Magnum" and the NRA classic, "If Guns Are Outlawed, Only Outlaws Will Have Guns".

Maybe Ned wasn't going to be so easy to work with after all.

And if Ned took that kind of attitude, what about the rest of his crew? Carla decided to show up first thing Monday morning to make sure they got off to a good start.

She turned left when she reached Broad Street and walked the extra two blocks to the delicatessen. She didn't have enough energy to do a regular grocery shopping and that meant cold cuts again for dinner. If Peter complained, she'd tell him he could start doing his share of the housework now that they were both working.

The deli was jammed with evening shoppers, but the manager gave her his full attention as she came through the door. "Ms. Weber," he cried, waving the cheese slicer he was holding. "Great to see you again."

Carla was startled. He'd never greeted her by name before. She was surprised that he even knew who she was. Then she realized what was happening. Her work for the Stauffers had made her an object of general interest.

"So how's it going over at the old Kettering place?" he demanded. "Making much progress?"

"The workmen start next week."

"Good, good. And what about the factory? Has Mr. Stauffer decided on a site for it yet?"

"Don't ask me. Owen and Bronwin don't keep me informed of their plans."

Carla realized she'd sounded terribly prim, but it didn't seem to put the man off. He stuck his knife in the hunk of cheese he'd been cutting and leaned over the top of the glass food case. "My brother-in-law is going to ask Mr. Stauffer for a job once the factory opens," he confided. It sounded as if his brother-in-law had been looking for work for a long time. There was a wealth of unspoken feeling behind the words.

The woman who was waiting for the cheese stirred restlessly. Carla assumed she was impatient to collect her order, but instead she joined the discussion. "My son is hoping to get a job with Stauffer Electronics, too. He'll be going off to college in a couple of years, and he's just got to find a way to make some money during the summers."

"Hey, Owen Stauffer hasn't made a formal announcement yet," Carla protested. "He may decide to keep the plant in Sacramento."

"Oh, no he won't." The shopkeeper's voice was confident. "Just wait until winter comes and he tries driving those icy roads down to the Valley. He'll move his factory up here real quick."

The delicatessen man went back to waiting on his customers, but he kept winking at Carla as she stood in line, as though they shared a wonderful secret. When her turn came, he put a couple of free dill pickles in with her order.

What was this, she asked herself as he handed her the package. Some badly thought out attempt at a bribe? She was hardly in a position to influence Owen Stauffer's business decisions. She decided not to question the gift, though. The delicatessen pickles were delicious.

Peter laughed when she mentioned the incident that evening over dinner. "You have a lot to learn about life in a small town. This isn't San Francisco, where everyone's from somewhere else. Except for the retirees—and a few lost souls like ourselves—people live here because they were born here, and that means they have relatives in the area. Practically every family in town stands to benefit from the factory."

"If Owen actually decides to build it. But why give pickles to me? I'm not going to provide them with jobs."

"No, but you work for Owen and some of the glamour rubs off." Peter took a big crunchy bite.

Carla didn't say anything, but she didn't like it. Owen was a nice guy, but he wasn't superhuman. They couldn't expect him to solve all of their problems. She couldn't shake the feeling that they were all of them, the whole town, riding for a fall.

Chapter 10

Ned was already hard at work when Carla arrived at the mansion first thing Monday morning. He and his four-man crew were clearing the drive, tearing out the small trees and bushes that had taken root in the gravel, so they could drive their trucks up to the house.

When they'd finished doing this, Ned's first priority was replacing the roof, to protect the house from further rain damage. The roof was one part of the mansion that couldn't be saved, he explained. It had been repaired too many times. Thousands of pounds of shingles and hot tar had been added over the years, and it had reached the point where the roof was so heavy it was threatening to wrench the house apart, forcing the walls out by its very weight. There was nothing to be done but tear the old materials off and start from scratch.

Demolishing the roof was a violent job. The men attacked it with hatchets. The work was incredibly dirty, too. Ned constructed a wooden chute leading to a debris box in the front yard and his men did their best to use it for the trash, but a tremendous amount of stuff inevitably fell to the sides. Shingles and scraps of roofing paper and small pieces of wood littered the grounds for fifty yards around, skittering across the rough grass whenever the wind blew. Even worse, from Carla's point of view, the greasy black grit from the attic made the most of its opportunity to escape. It sprang from every new hole, coating the grass and trees and bushes like a malevolent blight. Gallons of the filthy stuff made its way inside the house, where it proceeded to infest Carla's clothing, her hair, and even her teeth. The first thing she did when she got home every evening was to hurl her clothes into the washing machine and herself into the shower.

True to his word, Ned assigned Carla a helper. Rob Lawry was the youngest man on the crew, a weedy fellow in his late teens with lank hair and an overbite. He didn't have much to say for himself, but he was skillful at wielding a hammer.

They spent a full day cutting test holes in the walls. The evidence they uncovered confirmed Carla's guesses, and she was able to draw up the final set of floor plans.

Carla's work kept her busy. On top of that, she found that her after-work errands took twice as long to run. The experience at the delicatessen had been just a foretaste. Everyone in town was in a state of breathless anticipation, waiting for Owen Stauffer to make up his mind about the factory, and everyone was on the lookout for inside gossip. Strangers stopped her on the street to ask about Owen's plans, and she couldn't gas up Peter's car without getting involved in half a dozen conversations. Her work on the mansion was even bigger than the upcoming Pioneer Days celebration as a subject of general interest.

She didn't have much to tell her questioners except that Ned was making progress with the new roof. However, she picked up some news in her turn. Owen had joined the local rifle range and Bronwin had beaten Josie Kettering in the race for President of the Arts Center Board. Rumor was that Owen had made a contribution that was large enough to pay off the organization's budget deficit for the year.

Most of the people Carla talked to were strongly in favor of the factory, but some had reservations. The owner of the Conoco station summed it up one evening as he was making change for her. "Yes, an electronics plant would bring jobs to the area, and people would buy cars with their money, among other things. I'd sell more gas. But the Stauffers have really been throwing their weight around. I'm not so sure we need a couple of big city types telling us how to run our lives.

"Nothing personal, you understand," he added hastily, giving her a sideways glance. "If people want to move here, that's fine with me. But it seems like the Stauffers are kind of taking over."

Ned and his crew worked hard, and they finished tearing off the roof by the end of the week. They tacked down huge sheets of blue plastic to protect the house in case it rained over the weekend.

Trouble struck on Monday morning. Carla arrived for work to find Ned waiting at the front door. "I've got a new layer of paint to show you for your collection," he said grimly.

He led her to the dining room. A message was splashed on the wall in dark blue enamel, applied with a brush: "Stauffers Go Home!" The sign was at eye level, in ragged block letters about a foot high, and paint drips ran down to the floor.

"Back to Sacramento," the message continued helpfully in smaller letters among the paint drippings. The writer hadn't wanted the Stauffers to misunderstand and get the idea that they were being asked to confine their movements to their temporary quarters at the Mother Lode Lake house.

Carla put a hand to her mouth to restrain a giggle. Someone had finally gotten around to telling the Stauffers where they got off. Bronwin had had things her own way for far too long. She'd come here with her husband's money and snatched away Carla's house—or the house she wished were hers, to be accurate. Now

Owen was setting the town on its ear with his promise of new jobs—

The electronics plant! "My God, I hope Owen doesn't take this to heart," she blurted out. "We can't afford to lose the factory."

"I don't suppose Owen's thinking will be influenced by a bunch of young hoodlums." Ned dipped a rag in paint thinner and began to scrub at the paint, which was still tacky. He left a blue smear on the plaster but the words were still readable. "Kids! They aren't happy unless they're making a mess."

Carla looked at him doubtfully. She wasn't convinced he was right to blame the town's children. "Stauffers Go Home" was more of an adult phrase, reminding her of the "Yankee Go Home" signs the Europeans had scribbled on walls at the end of World War II. The principle was the same—the resentful inhabitants of a weak country telling a rich foreign power to leave them alone.

Ned's face grew worried. "I hope this was just a one-shot deal. I worked on a house in a rough part of Sacramento last winter, and the kids tore the place apart as fast as we could get it built. The owner finally had to hire a night watchman with a dog."

"Surely you don't have problems like that in a small town like Placer Bar."

"Oh, we have our share of vandals here. More than in the city, I sometimes think. There's nothing for the teenagers to do at night, so they ride around in cars looking for trouble."

"I suppose we ought to call Bronwin," he added. "She isn't going to be happy about this."

Ned had a cell phone. Carla used it to place the call. There was a moment of shocked silence when she finished talking. Then Bronwin snapped, "Hold everything. I'll be right over."

95

She got there in five minutes. She stared at the message for a long time, as if it had something to tell her hidden behind the actual words. Her fists clenched and a red flush spread slowly across her cheeks.

"My God, they really hate us here." She spoke softly, but there was pain in her voice. Carla was starting to feel sorry for her when she turned to Ned. "This is your fault," she snapped. "It's your responsibility to see that the house is secure. That's just basic when you take on a contracting job."

Ned seemed staggered by the accusation. "There's a dead bolt on the front door and another one on the back," he protested. "I've put nails in all the windows so they'll only open a few inches. What more do you expect me to do?"

Then a note of uncertainty entered his voice. "I'm sure we locked the house before we left for the weekend."

"You obviously forgot. Somebody got in."

Ned's face took on a mulish expression, but he didn't pursue the point. "Look, I'll double-check the locks tonight and I'll check all the windows, but if somebody really wants to break in, I won't be able to stop them. There's no way to keep people out of an empty house."

Bronwin glared at him without speaking, then turned on her heel and walked out. Ned looked at Carla and spread his hands. "I really don't think it was my fault."

"Bronwin's just upset," she murmured. "Leave her alone for a while and she'll simmer down."

She had to agree that Bronwin was being unreasonable. The house was vulnerable, particular so because it was in terrible shape. All the windows on the north side had been weakened by dry rot. Ned had nailed them shut, but she figured that a good strong tug would tear them loose from their frames.

"I just hope nothing else happens." Ned didn't sound opti-

96

mistic.

Things were quiet for a few days and it began to look as if the message on the wall had been an isolated incident. Then someone flushed a bag of concrete down one of the toilets on the ground floor. Carla had been working on the third story when it happened, and Ned's crew was still busy with the new roof, so the concrete had set by the time they discovered it.

"I'll call Bronwin this time 'round," Ned told her.

Bronwin didn't waste much time looking at the toilet. She had too much to say to Ned.

"If you want to keep your job, you're going to have to put an end to these acts of vandalism. I don't care what it takes, just do it!"

"I make sure the house is locked up tight when we leave." Ned couldn't keep the sulky tone out of his voice. "This time they broke in during the day."

"You're telling me they just walked through the front door? They pulled this stunt right under your noses?" Bronwin's voice was thin with incredulity.

"Well, yeah," he admitted, clearly on the defensive. "We make a lot of noise when we're working. We didn't hear a thing."

"Of all the incompetent idiots! I've spent a lifetime dealing with fools, but you take the prize!"

Carla left the room. She didn't want to listen to this.

It took Ned half a day to replace the toilet. He performed the work with an air of quiet fury. When he was finished, he called his men together and issued keys. He told them to keep the house locked at all times, even when they were going in and out carrying building materials.

"What can I do, short of posting an armed guard?" he asked Carla later. "I can't afford to lose this job, and if Bronwin fires me, it'll ruin my chances of getting work building the new factory. Owen Stauffer is going to be paying out a lot of money for that, and I've been counting on some of the cash ending up in my pocket." He half clenched his right hand, as if he were closing it around a pistol grip. "Maybe I ought to start camping out here at night. If the vandals come back, I'll give them a nasty surprise."

Carla remembered the National Rifle Association bumper sticker on his truck. "Think what you're saying. You told me it's kids we're dealing with here." She grabbed him by the shoulders and forced him to look at her. "You can't shoot someone for breaking into an empty house, much less a child. Anyway, what about your wife? What's she going to say if you start spending your nights away from home?"

"If she has to choose between that and the house we're planning to build . . ."

"Look, I'm sure Owen won't hold this against you. He seems like a reasonable man. He's in business himself, and he must have had a few experiences with Murphy's Law."

"Yeah. 'If anything can go wrong, it will.' That sure applies in this situation."

Carla looked at Ned helplessly. She really didn't think his job was in danger, but Bronwin had certainly succeeded in scaring him. She had to talk him out of this vigilante frame of mind.

"This isn't personal," she insisted. "Or if it is, you aren't the person the vandals are out to get. Those tricks were aimed at the Stauffers.

"That's what I can't understand," she went on. "Why would anyone want to chase the Stauffers out of Placer Bar? Half the people in town are counting on the new factory to bring money into the area."

"We're talking about kids. They don't think straight. The

Stauffers are a big deal right now—they're the main subject of conversation. Breaking into their house makes the kids feel important. They haven't stopped to reflect that in five or ten years, they'll need jobs themselves.

"Well, they haven't done any serious damage, and the precautions you've taken ought to slow them down. Leave it alone, okay? Even if worst comes to worst and you lose the job, it isn't worth committing murder."

"I guess," Ned said heavily.

* * *

The call came in the early hours of the morning. Carla was groggy and disoriented when she answered the phone and at first she didn't understand what Ned was saying.

"—more trouble on the job. You'd better get over here. Right now." He hung up before she could ask what had happened."

She turned on the light and got out of bed. Peter opened his eyes, yawning sleepily, and then sat up when he saw that she was putting on her clothes.

"What's going on?"

"Ned just called. Something's wrong at the Kettering mansion. It sounds serious."

"You can't go over there at this hour." He looked at the clock-radio. "My God, it's three o'clock in the morning!"

"He wouldn't have phoned unless it was urgent." She found a heavy sweater in the closet and thrust her arms through the sleeves.

"I guess I'd better go with you," Peter mumbled. He crawled out from under the covers and groped around on the floor for his slippers.

Carla had a bad feeling about this and it was growing stronger by the moment. The message in blue paint had struck her as funny, and even the concrete in the toilet had been nothing more than a colossal nuisance, but now she was beginning to feel afraid.

Chapter 11

Carla backed the Nissan out of the garage and waited, motor idling, while Peter got dressed. Why did he have to insist on going? She supposed she ought to appreciate his standing by her, but the delay was maddening. Fuming with impatience, she beat a tattoo with her fingers on the steering wheel. This was an emergency—God only knew what was happening at the mansion while she sat here waiting.

The wail of sirens revved up in the distance as Peter let himself into the car. Her skin prickled with fear. She threw the engine into gear and they shot forward before he had time to close the door.

"Watch it," he complained as the door slammed against his leg. He grabbed for the dashboard as she took the turn onto Ridge Road. She was driving much too fast and she barely made the curve without sending the car into the ditch. She forced herself to back off the accelerator; the last thing they needed was to get into an accident.

As they hurtled down the road, Carla remembered Ned's threat to stand guard at the mansion with his pistol. Had he put this plan into action—with terrible results? In her mind's eye, she saw the slim figure of a child slipping through the house, feeling its way in the dark. Ned, alerted by a noise, crawled out of his sleeping bag and went to investigate, gun at the ready.

"Stop!" he yelled, spotting a moving shadow, but the terrified youngster was too scared to obey. The kid came straight at him, hoping to escape. A running collision and the gun went off—

Carla wasn't sure if she was prepared to deal with this. She slowed instinctively, which was all that saved them when they rounded the final curve after the cemetery. The road in front was completely blocked by official vehicles: two fire engines, an ambulance and half a dozen police cars. Not to mention a number of private cars and trucks.

There was no place to park. She abandoned the Nissan in the middle of the road and took off at a run, Peter close on her heels.

Then she glimpsed a flicker of red through the trees. The mansion was on fire!

A small crowd had gathered in the road in front of the house to watch the leaping flames. Where had these people come from, she asked herself, at this late hour and in this deserted spot? Whatever they thought they were doing, they were in her way. She pushed her way toward the gates, forcing herself through the close press of bodies.

She finally broke clear of the crowd. The fire was at the back of the house. As best she could see in the dim moonlight, the facade was still unharmed. As she sprinted through the gate, a tongue of flame leaped roaring above the roof line.

Her eyes were on the fire and she collided with a cop who'd stepped forward to block her way. She tried to dodge around him, but he grabbed her arm. "You can't go in there, miss. You'll have to stand back with the others. You might get hurt."

He thought she was a rubbernecker, come to gawk at the flames. "I'm Carla Weber," she gasped. "I'm with the construction crew." She peered over his shoulder as she spoke. To her relief, the fire was still confined to the back of the building. Two fire engines had managed to make it down the drive before the street in front of the house was blocked by the abandoned cars of sightseers. One fire truck was parked in front of the mansion and its hoses snaked in through the open front door. The other had pulled up on the grass at the side of the house.

"No civilians. I have my orders. This situation is just too dangerous."

The cop was treating her like a child. Carla didn't have time to argue. Desperate, she resorted to begging. "Please, I've got to talk to Ned Fielding, the head of the work crew. He's probably the person who reported the fire in the first place. He'll tell you who I am."

"I don't care if you're Smokey the Bear. You're not going through these gates."

She hurled herself to one side, trying to jerk her arm free. She took the cop by surprise and almost succeeded in pulling loose from his grip.

"Hey, Brad!" he called, taking a fresh hold on her shoulders. "We've got a real firebug here. Better lock her in the back of the patrol car."

Carla stopped struggling and tried her best to assume an air of dignity. "There's no need for such measures. I came here to help, but I can see when I'm not wanted."

The cop didn't look happy about it, but he let her go. Peter was watching her from the edge of the crowd. "Come on," she said, grabbing his arm and propelling him ahead of her. "We've got to get back to the car."

The road behind Peter's Nissan had turned into a mini-parking lot during the time she'd wasted in the ruckus with the cop. The way in front was still impassable. To make things worse, more cars were arriving by the minute. Carla managed to turn around by putting the rear wheels into a ditch, probably wrecking the suspension, and finally, after an altercation with a burly man on a motorcycle in which she threatened to use her car as a battering ram if he didn't get his damn Harley out of the way, she worked the car back onto the open road.

"What's gotten into you?" Peter demanded as they roared toward town. "Honestly, Carla, I thought you were going to slug that cop when he refused to let you through the police line. Now you're ready to run people down just to get home!"

Carla pulled to a stop where the road arched over the creek. She cut the engine and handed Peter the car keys. "There's more than one way to reach the mansion. I'm going in from the back."

Peter threw his hands in the air. "We can't leave the car on the bridge!" he sputtered. "This is a 'No Parking' zone."

"I thought you could drive the Nissan home and wait for me."

The slam of Peter's car door echoed her own. "You really have lost your mind! I'm not about to let you go hiking across country at night by yourself."

Carla didn't reply. She was too busy scrambling down the rough path to the creek. Peter followed, complaining vociferously as he picked his way in the dim light cast by the solitary street lamp that lighted the bridge. "I don't get it. Why is it so important for you to reach the mansion? I mean, I'm glad to see you taking your new job so seriously, but aren't you carrying things a little too far? You're supposed to renovate the place, not save it from burning down. And that cop probably knew what he was talking about when he said the grounds were dangerous. You could be walking into serious trouble, and not just with the police." A worried note entered his voice. "Hey, are you sure you know where you're going?" They were down in the gully by now and it was awfully dark, the only light coming from the faint reflection of the moon on the rippling water.

"I know this stretch of the creek like the palm of my hand. I've fished it a dozen tiiiimes—shit!" She'd inadvertently strayed into the creek bed and her foot had slipped on a moss-covered rock. Agony seized her ankle. She hunched her shoulders against the pain and drew in her breath. "Maybe you ought to go back," she said in a kindly voice when she was able to speak again. "I'll be fine on my own."

Peter responded with a volley of curses, interspersed with the sound of crackling wood. It sounded like he'd blundered into a bush and was trying to tear himself free by main force.

"Peter can't you try to be a little quieter?" she snapped. "You sound like a herd of elephants back there."

"Hold on a minute. My damned coat is caught on this branch here—"

"I'll never be able to sneak past those cops with you blundering around. Can't you go back to the car and wait?"

There was a moment of silence. When Peter spoke, he was furious. "Back to the car, hell! You can do what you like. I'm going home."

The crashing noises receded back up the slope. Carla felt terrible about the way she'd treated him, but there wasn't time to worry about it now. The trail had given out and the underbrush was too thick to push through. Grabbing a willow branch that swung out over the water, she waded into the stream.

Five slogging, sloshing, slippery minutes later and she was crawling up the creek bank behind the house, muttering one of her usual lock-the-barn-door resolutions under her breath. She was going to keep a flashlight in Peter's glove compartment from now on, a powerful flashlight with fresh batteries. And she was going to start wearing heavy wool socks, the kind that insulate when wet.

She crouched behind a stand of buckbrush to reconnoiter. The red glare above the house had died down, and as she watched, the last few flames disappeared under the stream of water from the firemen's hose. Thank God, she told herself. The fire couldn't have done too much damage if they'd already managed to contain it.

A battery of blinding white lights sprang on, illuminating the rear of the house. Carla flinched back behind the bush and put up a hand to shield her eyes. Then it occurred to her that the cops would be dazzled too, for a moment, and she could take advantage of the glare to move in. She stepped out of hiding and walked quickly across the lawn, trying her best to look as if she belonged there.

The gathering in the back yard was a quiet one. The firemen had mounted powerful lamps in the lower branches of the trees and these provided spots of brilliant illumination. Men materialized and then disappeared again as they moved through the pools of light. Hoses snaked around the yard in random patterns, making the going treacherous in the darker parts, and the foul odor of smoke hung over everything.

Somebody adjusted one of the floodlights and Carla drew in her breath with a gasp of dismay. She could see the full extent of the damage now. The small reception room at the back of the house, the one with the fox hunting murals, had been destroyed. Nothing remained of the back wall except a few posts, still steaming, and the two side walls were almost completely burned away. What was left of the interior of the ruined room was black with smoke except for a small area near the door leading to the main structure. Some vagary of air currents had swept the smoke away from the wall, and one of the figures in the mural, a pink-jacketed rider taking a fence at full gallop, had escaped destruction. The hunter strained forward on his horse as if he'd been frozen in time, caught in the act of fleeing the conflagration.

Heartsick at the loss, Carla broke into a shambling run. At least the rest of the house didn't seem badly damaged, she tried to comfort herself. The main structure was still standing, blackened by smoke but unburned.

She'd been so busy worrying about the house that she'd forgotten about Ned. Now she caught sight of him standing over to the left. He was surrounded by a knot of men, most of them wearing police uniforms. A dark burly fellow in blue slacks and a brown sports jacket was yelling at Ned. He seemed to be very angry.

"How do I know how the fire started?" Ned's voice was thick with exasperation. "I was asleep. And I haven't had time to look into the matter, now that I've woken up. I've been too busy trying to stop the place from burning down."

"Ned," Carla called as she picked her way through the sprawl of fire hoses. The ground was wet and it squelched under her freezing, creek-numbed feet. As she drew nearer she could see that Ned's face and arms were crusted with soot, and his shirt hung off his thin frame in shreds.

"Carla! Thank God you've come. The cops won't listen to reason." He jerked a thumb at the man in the brown sports jacket, and she recognized Lieutenant Pressner. She gave the policeman a nod. He returned it, just barely, and turned back to Ned.

"I don't understand what you were doing out here at three in the morning," Pressner insisted. "Why weren't you home in bed? Fires don't just start by themselves, you know."

"My God!" Carla broke in. "You can't be suggesting that Ned's responsible. He's the last person—"

A man in a fireman's helmet pushed his way into their group. He was carrying a one-gallon gasoline can, suspended by a stick thrust through the handle. "It was arson, all right." He addressed Lieutenant Pressner as an equal. Carla gathered that he was someone fairly high up in the Fire Department.

"We found this gas can in a rose bush near the gate," he went on. "There's a lot of debris blowing around the yard and as far as we can tell, somebody gathered together a bunch of scrap lumber and piled it against the rear wall." He glanced at the burned-out shell of the sun room. "Then they drenched the wood with gasoline and set it alight. If there'd been any wind, the fire would have spread to the rest of the house. We were lucky to be able to contain this one."

He wiped the open spout of the can with his forefinger, then sniffed. "You can still smell the gas. Gasoline is volatile stuff, and it would have evaporated if this can had been empty for very long."

"Well, you can't blame Ned," Carla said firmly. "He's the contractor in charge of restoring the house and he needs the job. He'd hardly be likely to burn the place down." She turned to Lieutenant Pressner. "I can tell you what he was doing here. We've been having trouble with vandals. Somebody broke in and scrawled an insulting message on the dining room wall, and then they poured a bag of concrete down a toilet. Ned was acting as a watchman."

"This is the first I've heard of these incidents," Pressner said. "Why didn't you report them to the police?"

Carla shrugged. "What good would it have done? You wouldn't have detailed an officer to stand watch all night, every night. You don't have the manpower. That's the only thing that would have helped."

Pressner wasn't through with Ned. "So you're a contractor? And you're short on work? You wouldn't have been trying to drum up a little business, would you? This fire damage is going to cost a bundle to repair."

"You're Ned Fielding? The guy who called in the alarm?" The official in the fire helmet leaned forward and gave him a closer look. "Hey, you're the man who was hosing down the roof!" He turned to Lieutenant Pressner. "When we got here, he was up on top of the sun room, spraying water over the back of the house. He'd climbed up on the part of the roof that hadn't caught fire yet, playing a garden hose as high as it would go." The corners of his mouth turned down and he shook his head in reluctant admiration. "You have to be crazy to do a thing like that—but if you ever need a job, come talk to me. Ask for the Fire Chief."

A man in wheat-colored corduroy jeans and a matching jacket stepped out of the shadows. Carla didn't recognize Owen Stauffer at first in these casual clothes—or maybe it was his face that had changed. When she'd seen him previously, he'd struck her as an easygoing person, even a little diffident. Now his face was hard and angry.

He immediately took charge. "You're hurt," he told Ned. Then he raised his voice in a bellow. "Hey, we need a doctor over here!"

A short, balding man hustled over in response to this summons. He was dressed for the occasion in a white coat and he carried a large plastic case. He glanced around their circle inquiringly, and Owen jerked his head at Ned's arm. Carla realized with horror that the dark stains on his mangled sleeve were blood.

"Let's take a look at this." The doctor produced a pair of long-bladed stainless steel scissors from his fitted doctor's bag. He snipped at the remains of Ned's shirt. Ned went dead white as the doctor eased the material way. Ned caught a glimpse of a long black gouge surrounded by inflamed red flesh before she averted her eyes, sick to her stomach. Why hadn't Ned said something earlier? His injury looked serious.

The doctor sprayed the wound with an aerosol can. "We're going to have to take you to the hospital," he remarked in a conversational tone as he deftly rolled up the other sleeve of Ned's shirt and gave him an injection.

Ned, like the rest of them, hadn't realized how badly he was hurt. He must have been running on adrenaline. His face took on a glazed expression, as if the doctor had hypnotized him by calling attention to his wound. All the fight drained out of him; he followed the doctor toward the front of the house obediently.

Lieutenant Pressner rounded on Carla. "Okay, so your buddy's a hero. I still find it suspicious, his being here when the trouble started."

Owen cleared his throat. "I'm the owner of the property. I think it's possible that the fire was directed at me personally, that the arsonist wanted to drive me out of Placer Bar. I don't know if you've heard, but I'm planning to build a factory, and there's an element in town that doesn't like the idea."

Owen had been calm up to this point, but now his face twisted in fury. "Arson! What really galls me is the cowardice of the crime. If a man wants to stand up to me in public, that's fine, but sneaking around in the middle of the night setting fires is another thing entirely. Ned's been badly hurt, and he could have gotten killed. What kind of people do you have in this town, anyway?"

What Carla wanted to know was whether the fire had anything to do with the corpse she'd found in the linen closet. She couldn't shake the idea that there had to be a connection. The idea didn't make sense, though, she told herself. The murderer would hardly have set the fire hoping to destroy the evidence. Everyone in town knew that the body had been discovered and taken away. And even if the murderer had missed the news somehow, and come back thinking to dispose of his victim's corpse before the workmen discovered the body during the remodeling process, wouldn't it have been easier just to break in and steal the body? Why risk drawing attention to it by starting a fire?

Plus the fire had been set at the back of the house, and she'd found the dead man up front.

A sickening cloud of black smoke puffed up from the embers and Carla retreated, coughing. She was too tired and demoralized to think straight. All she wanted to do was go home. She would worry about the fire and the person who'd set it in the morning.

She pulled away from the small group and slogged around the side of the house in the direction Ned and the doctor had taken. The audience standing in the road had grown during her absence. Half the town seemed to have come out to watch the flames. She thought she recognized Maud's nephew standing in a clump of people next to the gate, and she noticed a familiar-looking woman hurrying down the road, away from the mansion. It was Pat Graedon from the Miner's Palace Hotel, her tall figure stork-like in a flapping raincoat.

The officious cop didn't think to question her, since she was coming from the direction of the house. She muttered a few words, face averted, and slipped by him without being challenged.

Their own house was dark when she finally reached home. Peter was in bed, but he was wide awake, and he turned on the bedside light as she slunk into the room. "Are you all right?" he demanded.

Carla hesitated, not sure how to reply. She felt like a cat just brought home from the vet's, wary, yet yearning to be comforted. She longed to throw herself into Peter's arms, but that would involve explaining why she'd been so determined to

111

reach the Kettering mansion. And she'd have to come up with a reason for treating him so badly. She decided to settle for a good night's sleep. "I'm fine," she said gruffly.

Peter wasn't in a mood for conversation, either. Reassured to learn that she was safe, he turned his back on her as she crawled into bed. She knew she was being weak, and putting it off couldn't possibly help, but she was relieved to be able to delay the inevitable discussion until later.

Chapter 12

Carla played possum the next morning, burrowing under the bedclothes and pretending she was still asleep. She figured the morning breakfast table was not the place to try to explain the way she'd behaved the night before. Peter must have agreed, for he didn't try to wake her up. He put his clothes on quietly and left the house, evidently deciding to pick up breakfast downtown.

When Carla heard his car back down the driveway, she snatched up the bedside phone. She dialed the hospital to check on Ned. He was making a good recovery, the admissions clerk told her, but they wanted to hold him another day for observation.

This raised the question of whether or not she should go to work, Carla reflected as she hung up. She supposed she should call Bronwin and ask. Surely Ned's crew wouldn't report to the mansion with him still in the hospital.

She threw on a pair of jeans and an old shirt and padded down the hall to the kitchen. She was struck by a new thought as she put the kettle on to boil. Owen had been very bitter about the arson attempt. It wasn't the damage to his property that had upset him so much as the way it had been carried out—and he'd seemed to blame the town and everyone in it, not just the arsonist. Maybe he was having second thoughts about moving to Placer Bar.

A rising excitement filled her as she sank down at the kitchen table, her hands gripping the coffee mug. If the Stauffers went back to Sacramento, that would put an end to the restoration project. The house would be empty again. Maybe she could buy it—well, no, she didn't have the money, even if they sold it at a bargain price. But it would be hers, all hers, to visit. She'd be able to go there whenever she liked.

Then she realized how ignoble this idea was. Her cheeks flushed with shame. She was practically siding with the arsonist, trying to twist his work to her advantage. What a contrast she was to Ned, who'd injured himself trying to save the mansion! But there was no getting around it; if Owen changed his plans, Bronwin would be out of her hair for good. Ned and his crew would go off to another job, allowing the house to slip back into its former state of peaceful neglect. She'd have its rooms and grounds all to herself again. It would probably take years for the Stauffers to find a buyer, especially considering the fire damage. She couldn't repress a shudder of satisfaction.

The longer she brooded over her morning coffee, the more the idea caught hold of her. She'd almost convinced herself that the Stauffers would be leaving when she put in the telephone call to Bronwin.

Her boss was quick to disabuse her. "Give up on the restoration project? Are you kidding? I have no intention of letting some bastard with a book of matches drive me out of town. Ned gets out of the hospital tomorrow morning and when he does, we're going right back on schedule. I intend to rebuild the sun room and everything. The insurance should cover the loss.

When we're ready, I'll hold an open house for charity. I hope the arsonist shows up for it. I want him to *choke* when he sees how beautiful the house is."

Her voice trailed off thoughtfully. "Of course, we may have trouble replacing the fox hunting murals."

"I've got some pictures that will help," Carla told her. "I went around the house with my husband's office Polaroid when I first started working for you. I thought I'd take before and after pictures. I documented the murals fairly thoroughly, so all you'll have to do is hire an artist to repaint them." Hell, she thought, she'd been hoping that Bronwin would abandon the house, and here she was encouraging her to go ahead with the restoration project. But she couldn't in all conscience hold back on the photographs.

Bronwin took her cooperation for granted. "Good work," she said. "So how's the wallpaper research going? I want to place the order next week."

The reproduction wallpapers would have to be specially printed, and the firm Carla had decided on required a month's lead time. She knew that Bronwin would have to decide on the patterns fairly quickly if the wallpapers were to be finished by the time Ned and his crew were ready to hang them.

"The job isn't going very well, I'm afraid. I've identified the original wallpapers for less than half the rooms, and I don't have a clue as to how the rest of the house was decorated." Carla explained about some of the problems she'd encountered. "Don't blame me. It's Davis Kettering's fault," she finished defensively. "He did things thoroughly, and that included steaming off the old wallpapers when it came time to redecorate."

"How unfortunate. What do you suggest we do?"

"I can borrow some nineteenth century wallpaper books from Port Costa Decorative Papers. They have an impressive library of old patterns. You can choose any designs you like for the rooms where I couldn't locate the originals, or I suppose you could even go with contemporary papers or paint."

"I suppose I'll have to settle for that, if it's the best you can do," Bronwin grumbled. "Still, I must say I'm disappointed." She hung up the phone.

Left with an unexpected holiday on her hands, Carla wandered into the spare bedroom. Bronwin was right, she hadn't done a thorough job on the project—the thought nagged at her. She took her knapsack out of the closet and carried it over to Peter's desk, where she sat down and pulled out the half-dozen scraps of original wallpaper she'd managed to find. The little folding ruler she'd discovered in the attic was lying in the bottom of the bag, and she took it out and fondled it absentmindedly as she examined her wallpaper collection. Not really thinking what she was doing, she ran her thumb over the score lines that divided the inches into fractions.

A faint roughness on the body of the ruler caught her attention. She snapped on the desk lamp. There was a black mark on one of the wooden pieces, oval in shape, too symmetrical to be dirt or a stain. She squinted, examining it carefully under the bright light, and she was just able to make out the stamped legend, "Whister's Hardware, Placer Bar".

The ruler had been a promotional gift from a hardware store—and it was just possible that it had been lost by one of the carpenters who'd built the mansion. It certainly looked old enough.

Carla ran for the phone book and thumbed through it. Sure enough, the firm was still in business. "Whister-Large Hardware" was listed in small type in the yellow pages. She scribbled down the address, then grabbed her purse and headed out the door.

Whister-Large Hardware was located on a back alley on the edge of the Historical District. The street hadn't been gentrified yet by charming shops catering to the tourists. The block was still a slum. Most of the other businesses seemed to be run-down garages specializing in bodywork and cheap car repairs. None of them looked very prosperous.

The hardware store didn't do much to improve the tone of the street. The facade hadn't been painted in years and the show window was so grimy, it was difficult to identify the goods on display. The glass in the front door was cracked. This must have been an accident, Carla surmised. No self-respecting burglar would think of breaking into this place.

A bell over the door jingled as she stepped inside. The only illumination came from the dingy front window. It took a moment for Carla's eyes to adjust, but then she saw that the room was lined with shelves holding tools and gardening supplies and kitchen utensils. Under the shelves were stacks of small wooden drawers, the type that hold different sizes of washers and screws. No bubble-packs here! Carla was delighted to see that she had found a real old-fashioned hardware store that sold nails by the pound, but her enthusiasm faded when she saw that the nails in the open bins were filmed with rust.

The place wasn't just dark, it was deserted. "Hello?" she called in a tentative voice.

She was answered by the sound of loud clapping, the enthusiasm of a large audience. It came from a closed door at the end of the shop. She lifted a flap and let herself behind the counter, then cautiously pushed the door open. The roar of many voices burst forth and she jerked back in surprise, letting go of the doorknob. The door creaked open.

She peered inside the room. Instead of the rowdy gathering of people she'd expected, there was one small man. He jumped up from his armchair and stared at her in fearful astonishment. Behind him was a television set tuned to a game show. The TV was playing at top volume.

"I didn't hear you come in," the man muttered, drawing a huge white handkerchief from his jacket pocket and blowing his nose to hide his confusion. By the time he was finished, he'd recovered his composure. "You must be a customer. What can I do for you?"

"Yes. No. That is, I'm not exactly a customer." She took a step into the room. There was a small cot in one corner, neatly made up, and a half-drawn curtain failed to hide a hot plate and a miniature refrigerator.

The shopkeeper tugged down the vest of his shiny suit in an attempt to hide a piece of shirttail that had escaped from his pants. "Not a customer." He sounded distinctly regretful. "I don't get a whole lot of business these days. Still, as long as you're here, maybe you'd like to look around. You must have a drain that needs a new stopper, or a picture you'd like to hang on the wall. I have a fine selection of picture hooks."

Carla was touched by his eagerness to sell her these small articles. "I'm sure I'll find something I can use, but first I'd like to talk for a moment. Are you Mr. Whister?"

"No, I'm Henry Large. The Whisters died out years ago. My father bought the shop from the last Mr. Whister when I was a boy. He kept the name because goodwill was included in the purchase price."

"I suppose I've come on a fool's errand. I'm trying to trace some goods that might have been sold here over a hundred years ago." Carla felt unreasonably disappointed. She should have realized that the shop would have changed hands. And even if Whister-Large Hardware had still belonged to the Whisters, it wouldn't have meant that a contemporary member of the family would have any answers for her.

She explained about the Kettering mansion and her search for the original wallpapers.

"Actually, I might be able to help you out." The man produced a pair of eyeglasses with heavy black plastic frames and perched them carefully on his nose. "My business records are a little disorganized at the moment, but if you're willing to do a little digging, you might be able to come up with something."

He led her through the shop to another door. This opened onto a small room next to the larger one he used as a home. He snapped on a ceiling light. "This is where I keep the books."

Both sides of the tiny office were lined with wooden filing cabinets, and a battered oak desk took up most of the remaining floor space. The top of the desk was buried under a thick sprawl of papers. A built-in wooden cupboard covered the rear wall of the room.

"Mr. Whister left his records behind when he sold the business to my father," Mr. Large explained. "I've kept everything. Thought it might come in handy if I were ever audited by the income tax people."

"I see." Carla was having trouble keeping a straight face. It was all too obvious that Mr. Large had never summoned up the energy to tackle the mess in his business office. His father must have suffered from the same lack of ambition.

"I'll leave you to it," he said, backing out the door. "I have a few things out front I ought to take care of."

He returned to his living quarters. The whinnying of horses and the sound of distant gunfire told her that he'd found a Western movie on the television.

Carla chose a file drawer at random and pulled it open. Four bulging grocery bags were crammed in the drawer, their tops folded over and stapled. She pulled off the staples with her fingernails and looked at the papers stuffed inside. The first bag held financial records for 1953, copies of receipts for goods the shop had sold and bills for expenses incurred. The other bags held papers dating respectively from 1962, 1963 and 1985. Evidently Mr. Large's system of bookkeeping was to let his records accumulate until it was time to prepare his taxes. When he'd filled out the forms, he would group the year's papers in a grocery sack and shove them into the nearest filing cabinet.

She felt sorry for any tax man who might be assigned the task of taking him on. Even an IRS agent didn't deserve such a fate. Of course, she mused, perhaps that was the idea. Maybe Mr. Large had a terrific grudge against the IRS and was just hoping they'd decide to audit him.

The bags weren't in any particular date order, but kept going back and forth in time as she worked her way down the row of file cabinets. This was a hopeless project, she told herself with gathering discouragement. The Larges had obviously saved every scrap of paper that their hardware store produced, but it was too much to hope that the Whisters would have been so compulsive.

She gave up on the file cabinets and turned to the huge wooden cupboard at the back of the room. She tried one of the doors and discovered a row of hardcover business ledgers. She opened the first book and her spirits soared. These were the business records of the original Mr. Whister, the one who'd done business with Davis Kettering. They had to be. The ledger dated from 1860.

Carla flipped through the pages eagerly. Every business transaction, whether buying or selling, was listed in chronological order in a neat copperplate hand. Most of the entries included the name of the customer the ancient shopkeeper had dealt with.

She skimmed through several of the ledgers searching for the Kettering name. When she finally found it, it was on a large order. The list of goods Davis Kettering had bought went on for eight pages.

As was common in the nineteenth century, the notes in the ledger were gratifyingly verbose. A typical entry on the Kettering order read, "3' x 3' plaster ceiling medallion for dining room, Sternholm Company garland pattern, paid for and on order 30 August 1864".

Unfortunately, the ledger wasn't quite so helpful when it came to wallpapers. It gave the names of the patterns but no descriptions: "Twenty rolls Fleur de Lys paper for upstairs sitting room". Carla knew the room this entry referred to, but she'd gone over the walls carefully and hadn't found any traces of a lily pattern wallpaper. There must have been hundreds of mid-nineteenth century wallpapers with a fleur de lys motif, so this didn't get them much further. Bronwin could choose one and know that she was approximately right, but it was still unsatisfactory.

"So near and yet so far," she sighed to herself.

She discovered the answer when she looked in the adjoining section of the cupboard. Mr. Whister had saved his old wallpaper catalogs, huge volumes holding actual samples of the papers listed in the account books. The cupboard had protected the catalogs from light and the colors were well-preserved. Carla located several of the wallpaper patterns she'd found herself, including the stripes and roses design from the little robing alcove under the stairs. The catalog sample was a lot cleaner than the scrap she'd salvaged from the house.

She gathered together the books she needed and knocked on Mr. Large's door. "I've found what I was looking for," she said, showing him the ledger and the catalogs. "Would you mind if I take these to a copy shop?"

"You can borrow them if you like." Then his smile grew doubtful. "Of course, it's always possible that I might be audited. You'd better leave your name and number so I can call you if I need the books back in a hurry." The tax man was very much on Mr. Large's mind.

She scrawled her phone number of the back of one of Peter's business cards. "I really appreciate your help. Oh, and before I go—I'd like to have a look around your shop, if I may."

He led her into the main room and turned on the overhead florescents. What she really needed was a garden hose, but the ones he had to offer looked too old to hold water. She settled for a galvanized tin watering can with a sprinkle spout and a beautiful pair of garden shears with ornate wrought iron handles. The shears could have been part of the first Mr. Whister's stock from back in the nineteenth century.

Mr. Large seemed pleased as he wrapped her purchases in a big sheet of brown paper, but he was uncertain how much to charge. He named a figure, apparently at random, then raised it when she insisted that she'd seen similar things at a higher price in another store in town. She was telling the truth, actually. She'd noticed some very expensive garden shears in the window of an antique shop.

"I'll come again soon and bring my friends," she called over her shoulder as she stumbled out the front door, burdened by her brown paper package plus the ledger and the wallpaper catalogs. "You have a lot of unusual items for sale."

A man was lounging against the brick front of one of the neighboring garages, smoking a cigarette. He glanced at the hardware store's grimy front window, then widened his eyes at her in a look of comic disbelief. She made a face back at him as she passed by on her way to Broad Street.

Chapter 13

Carla telephoned Bronwin as soon as she got home. She felt ridiculously proud of herself, considering the part that luck had played in her victory. But she'd gone the extra mile, she told herself. She couldn't keep a bragging note out of her voice as she explained how cleverly she'd tracked down the missing wallpapers.

"I think you'll be pleased with the patterns," she finished. "They're awfully pretty."

Bronwin wasn't as impressed as Carla would have liked. "You'd better show me the catalogs before you place the order with the wallpaper company. I don't want them to run off twenty rolls of a pattern I couldn't bear to live with. I'm free today—could you come by this afternoon?"

"Sure, I guess so. I'll have to ask Peter if I can borrow his car, but if that isn't a problem, I'll be there in half an hour."

Carla's elation faded as she hung up the phone. She'd worked herself out of a job, she realized with a sense of dismay. Her research was all but finished now, and this meant she'd lost her excuse for spending her days hanging around the mansion. Oh, she could still make the occasional inspection tour, check in to see how Ned and his crew were getting along, but they'd be through with the restoration work in a matter of months. Then Bronwin would move in and the house, in all its historically accurate reconstructed splendor, would be hers. She, Carla, would be lucky to receive the occasional dinner invitation.

Still, Bronwin was paying the bills, and her request to look at the catalogs was hardly unreasonable. Carla put in a call to Peter's office and arranged to collect the Nissan. She changed into a skirt—this was a business meeting, after all—and set off for the savings and loan parking lot, the spare set of car keys in her pocket and the catalogs and the ancient ledger cradled heavily in her arms.

Mother Lode Lake, where the Stauffers rented a house, was a new development of about two hundred houses grouped around a country club and a man-made lake, an upscale enclave that employed a guard at the gate to keep out unwanted visitors. The guard checked Carla's name against his list before giving her directions. She followed the road through several winding turns until she reached a cul-de-sac at the top of the highest hill in the subdivision.

The Stauffers's house was a huge low structure framed in natural wood siding, the redwood planks grown silver with exposure to the elements. The owner must have been glad to get the Stauffers as tenants even for a short-term rental, Carla reflected as she rang the bell. A good third of the houses she'd passed had wooden "For Sale" signs impaled in their browning and neglected front lawns.

Bronwin took her time answering the door. "Come on through," she said when she finally appeared. "I'm sitting out back near the pool." She was wearing shorts and a halter. Carla thought it was interesting to see her slopping around the house like a normal person, for a change.

This was the first time Carla had been to the house, and she glanced around curiously as Bronwin led her through the living room. The decor was stark in the extreme; bleak, even, in its severity, with white walls towering up to a cathedral ceiling. Cream-colored sofas and chairs sat on a vast expanse of white carpeting like so many snow forts, and even the end tables were made of glass and pale bleached wood. Abstract paintings in harsh primaries provided the only spots of color. Carla wondered if Bronwin had chosen the furnishings herself—and she also wondered if the furniture came with slipcovers in a warmer shade. The room was cold looking in the summer heat, and it would be unbearable in winter with snow on the ground.

Bronwin pushed aside a sliding glass door leading to a redwood deck. A flight of stairs attached to the back of the house took them down to a swimming pool embedded in a stretch of green lawn. With its hilltop location, the house had a magnificent view of the surrounding mountains and the man-made body of water in the center of the development.

Bronwin flopped down on a yellow plastic chaise longue, dislodging a glossy fashion magazine which fell to the orange and blue tiled swimming pool surround. She retrieved the magazine and put it with a stack of others on a small wire table next to the chaise, weighing the pile down with a smooth rock with a happy face painted on the front of it. "Help yourself to a beer or something," she said, waving in the direction of a set of folding doors closing off the underside of the deck.

Carla handed her the books, then pushed the nearest door aside to disclose a utility room housing a hot water heater and pool pump and a spare refrigerator. The refrigerator was stocked with nothing but drinks—alcoholic and non-alcoholic, regular and sugar-free, carbonated and still. Carla hadn't even heard of some of the soda brands, and all of the wines looked expensive.

She popped the cap off a Corona beer and wandered back to the tiled area. There was only the one chaise longue, so she pulled up a plastic folding chair. Her hostess was leafing through the wallpaper catalogs in a desultory manner. Bronwin usually seethed with a sort of unpleasant energy, but today she seemed tired, almost listless.

Carla pointed out the wallpapers that had been used in the Kettering mansion, but Bronwin's face remained expressionless. "Well, what's the verdict?" Carla demanded. "Are you going to veto any of the designs?"

"They'll do, I guess." Bronwin tossed the books down on the end of the chaise. Carla winced to see her handling the fragile old volumes as carelessly as she'd treated the fashion magazine. "You've done a good job," she added with a complete lack of animation. "I'll mention this to Owen. He may want to give you a bonus."

"It was a stroke of luck, finding the hardware store. Still, it's good to know that our restoration job will be authentic in every respect."

"Oh, that house." Bronwin lay back and closed her eyes against the sun. "I'm beginning to wish we'd never decided to move to Placer Bar. It was Owen's idea, you understand. He's the one who's so hot for the small town life. He grew up near San Jose when the place was still a farm town, before it mushroomed into the world capital of the computer industry. I think he's hoping to recreate the simple days of his childhood here in the Sierra foothills. For a sophisticated businessman, he has a big naive streak."

Despite her lack of energy, Bronwin seemed to be in a mood for conversation. "Where did you grow up?" Carla asked.

"Chicago. The slums of the North Side."

Carla was a little surprised. She hadn't really thought about it, but she would have assumed that Bronwin was from an upper-middle class background.

"Chicago was a city, at least," Bronwin went on, her voice

taking on its familiar aggressive edge. "It had people, places to go, things to see, as they say. I moved to San Francisco thinking I'd expand my horizons, and now where do I find myself? In this Godforsaken little town. There aren't even any minorities here, have you noticed? Everybody's the same color and everybody thinks the same way."

Carla reflected that she ought to sympathize with Bronwin's frustration—after all, she herself was frantic to get back to the Bay Area—but there was something about the other woman that brought out the devil's advocate in her. "You haven't done much to explore the town's possibilities," she said. "If anything, you've gone out of your way to alienate people. Take Josie Kettering, for example."

Bronwin's mouth twisted in a smile of malicious amusement. "Oh, Josie. She's a big frog in a small pond, and I do mean frog! She swells up when she gets angry, have you ever noticed? It's fun to watch. Her eyes bug out and you almost expect her to start croaking."

"What made you decide to run against her for President of the Arts Center?"

"I wanted to see her swell up like a frog." Bronwin widened her eyes, playing the innocent, but her voice was mocking. "She was so sure she'd be reelected that she didn't even bother to campaign—and you should have seen her face at the meeting when they counted the votes. She doesn't deserve the job, anyway. She's been the President since everyone can remember, and she took the position for granted. She hasn't had an original idea in years. Not that I intend to do much work promoting the local artists, but at least I won't make a worse President than Josie Kettering."

Carla took a quick swig of her beer to hide her amusement. There was something refreshing about Bronwin's lack of pretense, especially after the devious and hypocritical way she her-self had been acting recently. Bronwin was abrasive, but at least she was honest about her feelings.

"Then there's Pat Graedon," she continued, curious to find out what her hostess would say about the hotel keeper. "At Josie's tea party, you seemed to be doing your best to antagonize her."

"Pat's a different story. I feel kind of bad about her. Owen tells me that she and her husband have invested every penny they have in that fancy bed-and-breakfast. It's their life's dream to make a success of the place. She really believes that Owen's fac-tory is going to drive them into bankruptcy, and who knows—maybe she's right. It will definitely bring a little hustle and bustle to this sleepy town. Still, there's not much I can do about it. If I had my way, Owen would move the factory to San Fran-cisco, or Los Angeles—to any big city, I don't really care which one. But you can't expect Pat to take a shine to me under the circumstances."

Carla was about to mention Sally Bolt, but then she remem-bered her suspicion that Sally might be taking a romantic inter-est in Bronwin's husband. If she was, Bronwin would probably be aware of it—she didn't seem to miss much. She decided to leave the subject of Sally alone.

"What about Maud Rucker?" she asked instead. "She's in favor of the factory, but you don't seem to like her very much."

"Are you serious?" Bronwin's eyes flew open. "That old bat! She and that nephew of hers are living in the past—or in never-never land, that's more like it. A gold claim on Casitas Creek! I've never heard anything so ridiculous in my life."

Carla stiffened. Bronwin had managed to get to her at last. She liked Maud, and she didn't appreciate hearing her dismissed as a fool.

Perhaps sensing that she had lost her audience, Bronwin sat upright again and began leafing through the old ledger. She ran a carefully manicured finger down the first page of the Kettering order and her eyes sharpened with interest. "You really have done a terrific job here. This deserves a celebration. I know— I'll throw a pre-housewarming party this weekend. Actually, my husband may have an important announcement to make." Bronwin closed the book, leaving her finger between the pages to mark her place.

It sounded as if Owen had made a definite decision to move his factory to Placer Bar, and Bronwin would be giving the party so he could tell the townspeople about his plans. The thought didn't do much to cheer Carla up. They'd never get rid of the Stauffers now. She rose to her feet and began to gather together the old wallpaper catalogs. Her earlier unhappiness had returned in full force.

"Leave the books here with me," Bronwin said sharply. "I want to show them to Owen. I'll give them back to you next week so you can order the reproduction wallpapers." She took the heavy volumes from Carla and put them on top of the stack of magazines, then rose to her feet and led her up the stairs to the deck.

The thought of throwing a party seemed to have restored Bronwin's spirits. She was clearly eager for her guest to leave so she could start making plans. She hovered impatiently while Carla fumbled with the front door lock, then waved a hasty goodbye as she left the house.

Chapter 14

The invitation to the Stauffers' party arrived the next day, delivered by hand by a high school boy that Bronwin had hired as a messenger. The Stauffers were certainly making a big thing out of this, Carla reflected as she read the formal message on a card of heavy paper: "The pleasure of your company is requested for cocktails on Saturday evening, at the hour of six o'clock."

She was in no mood to celebrate, but at least Peter would be pleased. She'd told him that Owen would be making an announcement, and he'd been driving her crazy with his interminable speculations about when the factory would finally open for business.

They accepted the invitation, of course, but an emergency phone call from Peter's boss delayed them, and it was almost seven o'clock by the time they reached the Stauffers's house. The white-on-white living room actually looked good with a crowd of people in it, Carla noticed as she handed her shawl to the tuxedo-clad rent-a-butler at the door. This was the way the room was meant to be seen, as a backdrop for the women's bright dresses and the dark suits of the men.

As Carla had guessed, the real purpose of the party was to inform the town of Owen's business plans. Owen, flushed and beaming, stood next to a table bearing an architect's scale model of the factory building. Bronwin held court at his side, gorgeous in a long narrow gown covered with silver sequins. Her husband looked genuinely happy and excited, but Bronwin's smile held a mocking edge.

Carla and Peter went over to pay their respects, and she looked over the architect's model while they waited their turn in the informal reception line. She could tell by the curve of the artificial river that Owen had bought the lot he'd been inspecting earlier, the site of Steve Rucker's "claim". The factory itself was a rather dull-looking building of the cement slab type, the kind where the walls are cast in the earth and then raised into position by giant cranes.

Carla was already demoralized, and the display made her feel even worse. The factory model was an all-too-real incarnation of Owen's plans. Once they'd built the plant, the Stauffers would be a permanent fixture in Placer Bar, impossible to dislodge. It would put an end to the possibility that the mansion would ever be Carla's.

"—scheduled for completion in late March or early April," Owen was telling the admiring crowd, mostly men, that jostled around him.

Carla couldn't stand it any longer. She grabbed a glass of punch from the tray of a passing waitress and plunged blindly for the far side of the room, desperate to get away from Peter before she burst into tears.

Most of the guests were strangers, she noticed when she'd recovered herself a little. They were Owen's business associates from Sacramento, or people from the Arts Center or the rifle range. Surprisingly, Bronwin had also invited a number of her local adversaries, probably because she wanted to throw her husband's success in their faces. Carla wondered briefly why they'd accepted, but then she decided they just couldn't keep away. Like herself, they were determined to torture themselves by witnessing the final defeat of their hopes.

Maud Rucker stood near the sliding glass door leading to the rear deck. She was talking with great animation to an elderly gentleman, and for a change she wasn't eating anything. Her nephew was there too, lurking in a corner. He was neatly dressed in a clean plaid shirt and new blue jeans and he even sported a yellow knit necktie, but he looked out of place among the other men in their dinner jackets and well-cut business suits.

Carla was intrigued. Steve Rucker was the last person she'd have expected to find at the party.

He started and whirled to face her when she walked up behind him. "I thought you and Owen were feuding over that lot near the creek," she said bluntly. "You couldn't resist coming to his victory celebration, huh?"

Steve's face turned bright red. "Owen's not such a bad guy once you get to know him." He hesitated. "Actually, I wouldn't be surprised if we came to some sort of arrangement about my claim." He backed up a few paces, then turned and bolted in the direction of the bar.

She stared at his retreating back, wondering what he'd meant by that last remark. Did he think Owen was going to let him dredge for gold on the factory grounds?

Or maybe he was hinting at some sort of shakedown attempt. Did he think he could get Owen to pay him not to enforce the "Code of the West"? Carla had seen cases of legal blackmail where people brought nuisance lawsuits for the sole purpose of extracting money from their victims, figuring the people they were suing would find it cheaper to pay them off than to fight it out in court. But you needed some semblance of a case to begin with, and Steve didn't have that. She doubted if he would even manage to find a lawyer to represent him, assuming this was what he had in mind.

Well, it was nothing to do with her. She knocked back the remaining inch of punch and exchanged her glass for a full one from a tray standing on a side table.

She caught sight of Ned Fielding as she started on her second drink. He was standing by himself, isolated in a small cleared space in the middle of the room. She waved a greeting and he drifted over to her side. Ned had been gloomy and depressed since the night of the fire, and at the moment he looked as if someone had just told him that his dog had been run over.

"Hi, Ned." She mustered a smile, hoping to cheer him up. "Did you bring your wife?"

"Naah. She's home with the kids. I thought I ought to put in an appearance, for a few minutes at least, but there wasn't any reason to drag her along to this funeral."

Carla was about to question his choice of words to describe the party, and protest that she'd been looking forward to meeting Mary Fielding, when she realized that Ned wasn't paying any attention to her. His eyes were on Owen, who'd separated himself from the group of admiring businessmen and was heading out the front door. Ned had a peculiar expression on his face, as if the punch he'd just swallowed had left a sour taste in his mouth.

The door shut behind Owen and Ned glanced back at her, remembering his manners. It occurred to Carla that he might have some idea about what Steve Rucker had in mind. "Do you know that guy?" She nodded at Steve, who'd managed to get a real drink out of the overworked bartender. He was standing propped against the wall with his legs crossed, gulping the amber liquid as if he was trying to work up a case of Dutch courage.

"Sure. Steve's the town nut. Says he's found gold in Casitas Creek."

"I think he might be trying to extort money from Owen."

"Good luck to him, if that's what he's after." There was a strong note of bitterness in Ned's voice. He grabbed a couple of fresh punch glasses from a passing waitress and handed one to Carla.

Carla's attempt to lighten her friend's mood with idle talk obviously wasn't working. "Is something wrong?"

"No, no, nothing at all." Ned wasn't very good at sarcasm. "It's just that my last hope of getting work building the factory went up in flames along with the sun room at the back of the mansion. I ran into Bronwin when I first got here, and she gave me a dirty look. I'll be lucky if she doesn't hire someone else to finish doing the work on the house. She thinks I'm incompetent, and I know she's got her husband convinced of it, too. I told him how much I admired the factory model and he just thanked me. He didn't say a word about his construction plans."

"Well, you can hardly expect Owen to talk business now. He's throwing a party. He'll probably call you in a day or two and invite you to submit a bid." Carla's voice wavered on the last few words. She wondered if Ned was right, and he'd lost his chance of getting any more work from the Stauffers.

"I'm not counting on Bronwin and Owen for much of anything right now." Ned wandered off morosely before she could reply.

Left on her own again, Carla grabbed a fresh drink while she scanned the crowd for familiar faces. Pat Graedon was standing near the front door, deep in conversation with Josie Kettering. They were with a man that Carla recognized from Josie's photograph album as Howard Kettering, her husband, although he was a lot older than he'd been in the pictures. She

135

went over to say hello.

"—just terrible," Josie was wailing as Carla approached. "Placer Bar has always been such a peaceful community. It's hard to believe that anything so awful could have happened here."

"The fire was only the beginning," Pat Graedon snapped. "We'll be seeing a lot more of that kind of big city trouble if Owen goes ahead with his factory plans. Urbanization, that's what it all comes down to. The Stauffers are going to destroy our peaceful small town atmosphere."

"Oh, come now," Howard broke in. "The fire had nothing to do with the factory. It was set by kids, I think we're all pretty much in agreement on that. Local teenagers, looking for kicks."

"Vandalism is nothing new around here," Carla told them as she joined the group. "Ned Fielding tells me he's seen a lot of it." She remembered Josie's story about the pranks she'd pulled as a kid, like moving Maud's outhouse to the middle of Broad Street, but decided this was not a good time to bring up the subject. Josie probably put her own behavior in a different category, anyway, seeing it as cute rather than malicious.

Josie stared at her blankly for a minute, then recovered herself. "Carla this is my husband, Howard Kettering."

Carla smiled to acknowledge the introduction and continued her thought, her eyes flicking to Pat Graedon. "From what Ned says, the kids in this town can play pretty rough."

Pat sniffed and drew back, distancing herself. Josie looked at Carla a little wildly. "Well, I think it's horrible that children should be so vicious and destructive. I can understand harmless jokes like soaping windows on Halloween, but setting fires— honestly! I hear Ned Fielding was asleep in the house when it happened. He could have been killed—" Her voice trailed off in a wail. Carla noticed that her face was flushed and her glass was

136

empty.

"That's the terrible thing about arson," Howard announced sententiously. "It doesn't just harm property. All too often, it leads to fatal accidents."

"Well, at least the fire hasn't stopped Owen from bringing his factory to Placer Bar." As she finished speaking, Carla realized the effect her words would have on Pat Graedon. She felt sorry about this; she didn't want to make her unhappy.

"It's all very well for you to talk." Pat narrowed her eyes. "You're an outsider and you have no real stake in this town. But there are some of us who are trying to build our lives here, who think Placer Bar is a special place. We don't want to see that specialness destroyed."

"How are you getting along with your petition?" Carla asked hastily, trying to make up for her tactlessness. "Have you gathered many signatures?"

Pat sighed. "I've given up. People keep telling me they'd *like* to sign, but they figure it's a lost cause. Owen has too much money and too much influence for people like us to stop them. They say we can't prevent big industry from coming here, so we might as well make the best of it. What they mean is, they're afraid of antagonizing Owen. They don't want to make an enemy of him by going on record against his precious factory."

Josie gave Carla an offended look, as if she linked her with the resented Stauffers. Howard Kettering was the only person in the group who wasn't annoyed with her at this point. "Yes, there's nothing to stop Owen now," he told them, evidently pleased at the thought. "He's bought that lot he was angling for, and the blueprints have been okayed by the Planning Commission. Now all he needs is approval from the City Council, and that'll be pretty much a rubber stamp procedure, as I understand."

"Try and find me a gin and tonic, will you, darling?" Josie handed Howard her empty punch glass. "I've had enough of this swill." She linked arms with Pat Graedon and drew her aside as her husband obediently turned and headed for the bar.

She'd put her foot in it with Pat and Josie, Carla reflected, feeling somewhat abashed. She decided to look around for Peter. Maybe he could help her keep her tongue under control.

People were beginning to leave and the room was much less crowded. Her husband was easy to find. Owen Stauffer had returned from his errand, whatever it had been, and Peter was standing with the group buzzing around the hero of the evening. Bronwin was nowhere in sight, and Carla was amused to see that Sally had taken her place at Owen's side. "I think it's fantastic," she was telling him. "First you fix up the old Kettering place, and now you're solving our unemployment problem single-handedly." She gazed with adoration into Owen's eyes. "You're really shaking this town out of its rut."

Carla experienced an overwhelming impulse to giggle. She covered her mouth with her fists, trying to disguise her laughter as a cough. What had Bronwin put in that punch, she wondered. And how many glasses had she finished? If she didn't watch out, she was going to make a fool of herself.

She jumped as somebody came up beside her. Maud Rucker was looking meaningfully at Sally and Owen.

"Those two have become an interesting item," the old lady announced with relish. "They've been causing a lot of talk down at the Gun Club. Sally's a member, but she stopped going after her husband died. Then Owen joined and she rediscovered her enthusiasm for banging away at paper targets. Somehow the two of them always manage to show up for target practice on the same day."

138

Carla thought about this for a moment. "Well, it can't be a serious romance." She realized her voice was a little woozy, but she went on aggressively. "I mean, surely if they were sleeping together they wouldn't be so obvious about it. This is an awfully small town."

"You never know. Some people aren't very subtle. And who can say it isn't for the best? Sally might make Owen a real good wife. That Bronwin just doesn't seem to fit in here." Maud shook her head in amiable disapproval and headed off in the direction of the buffet table, leaving Carla with something new to ponder.

The Kettering mansion was Bronwin's project. Owen had told her straight out that he wasn't all that enthusiastic about moving into the place. If the Stauffers got divorced, surely Bronwin would leave town—and despite her interest in local history, Sally probably wouldn't want to live in the old house. Judging from what she'd seen of her friend's living arrangements, Sally's taste in domestic architecture ran towards the modern. Owen could move in with Sally or they could build a new house. But whatever they did, the Kettering mansion would be left empty again.

Somehow in the course of this pipe dream, Carla had managed to acquire and finish a new drink. She gazed sadly into her empty glass. This scenario was all very well, but it depended on Owen's getting rid of Bronwin. And Bronwin wouldn't be an easy woman to get rid of if she didn't want to go.

She decided to forget about Peter for a while and walk out on the deck for some fresh air to clear her head. She pushed aside the sliding glass door. The deck lights had been turned off and the redwood platform was deserted.

The punch had given her a slight headache. She leaned on the rail and gazed down at the lake, far away at the foot of the hill, and abandoned herself to a mood of melancholy.

She didn't know how long she'd been standing there, a minute at least, when a spark of light brought her back to the real world. Her vision blurred and she squeezed her eyes shut, giving herself a little shake. When she opened her eyes again, she found herself looking down at the last gleams of late summer sunlight on the waters of the lake. She shivered again, more violently this time. She was in no mood to return to the party.

She felt her way down the shadowed stairs, drawn by the bubbling of the small spa attached to the pool. She crossed the tiled area and stared down into the dark, rolling water, trying to sort out her thoughts.

Then she raised her head and looked across the spa to the pool. A silvery shape floated on the surface. Long blond hair and the glittering sequined fabric of a dress were clearly visible in the fading light.

"Bronwin?" she whispered, nervously licking her lips. What was Bronwin doing in the pool, she asked herself stupidly, trying to deny the knowledge that this meant serious trouble.

Then she realized that Bronwin was floating face-down. "Help!" she screamed. She ran across the grass and took a flying leap into the water.

Chapter 15

Carla wasn't dressed for lifeguard duty even if she'd possessed the skills, which she didn't. Her full chiffon skirt immediately filled with water and wrapped itself around her legs in a vise-like grip. She grabbed the pool gutter with one hand to keep from drowning as she clawed the clinging material up around her hips until she could tie most of the fabric in a rough knot. Then she struck out for Bronwin, who was floating in the center of the pool.

She had to get Bronwin's face out of the water. She grabbed her far arm and tugged frantically, trying to flip her over onto her back. This proved impossible. Bronwin's muscles were limp, and her body was heavy and difficult to control. She plunged down and then shot forward, almost escaping from Carla's grasp.

After a few moments of useless struggle, Carla decided that the only thing to do was to drag her to the shallow end. Lifting Bronwin's head up was the main thing, and once she could use her feet for leverage, she ought to be able to prop her against the side of the pool.

She grabbed Bronwin by the hair and started swimming, side-kicking awkwardly, making the best speed she could, but it was a terrifyingly slow process. For such a slim woman, Bronwin possessed a tremendous amount of inertia. It was a struggle to get her going, and even once she had the body in motion it exerted a heavy drag.

They finally reached a spot where Carla could touch bottom. The job went a little easier after that, but she was sobbing and gasping for breath by the time she'd pulled the still figure to the shallow end of the pool.

She bent down and heaved with all her strength, finally managing to flip Bronwin over. Then she tried to push her into a sitting position, with her head up and her back against the concrete side of the pool. Bronwin's legs immediately popped to the surface and down she went again, head under water. She slipped from Carla's grasp and headed slowly feet-first in the direction of the deep end.

This was horrible, like trying to cram a giant jack-in-the-box back into its container. An obstinate toy with a super-powerful spring. Carla grabbed Bronwin's shoulders and managed to propel her back against the side of the pool again. Corralling the body with her arms, she took a firm grip on the shallow gutter and jammed both her knees into Bronwin's stomach, bracing her against the concrete by sheer force. Bronwin's mouth fell open and a thin trail of water dribbled down her chin.

"Carla, what the hell are you doing in the swimming pool? What do you think this is, La Dolce Vita?" Peter's footsteps boomed on the stairs that led down from the deck.

She tried to respond but no words came out, only a weak mewing sound like a kitten in distress. Holding Bronwin up out of the water took all of her remaining strength.

Then Peter realized she was in trouble. "My God!" he gasped. He raised his voice in a shout, much louder than the one Carla had managed to produce. "Help!" He jumped into the pool, raising a sheet of water that washed in and out of Bronwin's slack mouth. "You take that side. We'll lift her out together when I give the signal," he told her. "Okay, heave!"

Before she could obey, the deck lights came on. There was a loud clamor of voices and then the sound of many feet on the wooden staircase. Suddenly the pool was surrounded by people, all the guests who were still at the party, it seemed like. Most of them realized that it was Bronwin who needed saving, and they tugged at her arms and her dress, but a couple of the men grabbed Carla and forcibly pulled her out of the water.

Now that help had arrived, Carla was content to creep back into the shadows by the stairs while the others, led by Steve Rucker of all people, tried to revive Bronwin. She watched in despair as Steve started mouth-to-mouth resuscitation on the limp figure laid out at the side of the pool. Carla knew his efforts were hopeless. She'd accepted the truth when Peter had taken over the rescue effort. Bronwin was dead.

And not by accident. She'd sobered up by now and there was no doubt in her mind what had happened. She, Carla, had killed Bronwin in a fit of drunken madness. Evidently she'd stabbed her, with a shiny knife. What else could the silvery glitter have meant, the sparkling light she'd seen just before she ran down the steps? She'd stabbed Bronwin and then thrown her into the water. She'd wanted to get her rival out of the way, and she'd gone about achieving this in the most direct and brutal way possible.

Carla was shivering as the night air struck through her clammy gown. Now she flushed hot with shame, as she realized that she'd tried to excuse her inexpressibly evil action by denying it. She had no memory of killing Bronwin, or of the events that must have taken place immediately before and after the murder. She was a killer, and she didn't even know exactly what she'd done. She grew sick with self-loathing as she thought about this incredibly stupid attempt to evade responsibility.

Sierra Gothic

The fact that she couldn't remember made her frantic. She tried desperately to reconstruct what must have happened. She'd wandered out onto the deck, that much was certain. She drifted over to the rail where she—she glimpsed Bronwin? Bronwin must have been standing by the pool, or perhaps she was lying on her chaise longue. The sight of her enemy waiting alone and unprotected must have done something terrible to her mind.

Carla's throat worked convulsively as she tried to force down the bile that threatened to flood her mouth. This was disgusting. How could she have done such a thing? She wished with all her heart that she hadn't, that poor Bronwin was still alive.

But there was no undoing the evil deed. Trying to block out the guilt, she forced her thoughts back to the mechanics of the murder. Okay, she'd been standing on the deck. Unarmed, presumably. Come to think of it, where *had* she gotten hold of the knife? Moving like an automaton, she must have gone back into the house to find a weapon. The kitchen was the logical place to look, so she'd probably gone there. She'd opened a drawer and found what she was searching for. Knife in hand, she'd stolen back to the deck, down the steps, and then crept up behind her victim and stabbed her in the back.

Wait a minute, she checked herself. Her reconstruction didn't fit the facts. She had a vivid visual memory of Bronwin as she'd looked when she jumped into the pool to save her, and there was no blood on Bronwin's dress. She'd been a clean silvery shape, strangely peaceful-looking as she floated face down on the dark water.

That meant she'd attacked Bronwin from the front. The other woman would have put up a struggle, and she, Carla, would have been drenched in blood. She glanced down at her hands and dress, searching for evidence to confirm this. Her skirt had come unknotted by this time and it flapped wetly against her legs, but she didn't see any rips or stains. Had Bronwin's blood washed off when she jumped into the swimming pool?

Then she remembered the moment when the men drew Bronwin from the water. The lights had been on and she knew she couldn't be mistaken: The front of Bronwin's dress had been unmarked. There was no blood in this picture, either.

Just how *had* she murdered the damn woman? Pushing her into the pool wouldn't have done the job. Bronwin wasn't helpless, she would simply have climbed out. She must have stabbed her somewhere! Carla gripped her temples with the heels of her hands. Why couldn't she remember?

Well, forget about the murder method for the moment. She'd find out soon enough, no doubt. What happened next? She must have disposed of her weapon in some way, thrown the knife in the pool or hidden it in the bushes. She'd returned to the deck and come out of her murderous fugue state, or whatever you wanted to call it. She hadn't even felt guilty. Instead, she'd lounged around as if nothing had happened, falling into a self-pitying funk.

Then she'd been horrified when she saw the dead body. She'd run down the stairs to stage a rescue attempt. What on earth had she been thinking when she pulled that one? Did this indicate a change of heart, or was it merely some despicable subconscious plan to wash off the incriminating bloodstains? Carla suspected the latter. She was hardly in a position to believe anything good about herself.

The sound of emergency sirens swelled louder, and now the vehicles began drawing up in front of the house, emitting their last surly whines. A small army of men stormed down the deck stairs. Carla recognized the doctor who'd tended Ned's injured arm on the night of the fire. Lieutenant Pressner was right behind him.

The police. Oh, no! It suddenly burst in on her that the murder she'd committed was bound to have legal consequences. If Pressner learned she was the killer, she'd be sent to jail. For a long, long time.

No! She recoiled in horror from the prospect. She was deeply sorry that she'd killed Bronwin, she'd give anything if she could only bring her back to life, but she didn't want to go to prison. She had to find a way out of this.

Carla shrank still further back into the shadows under the deck as the cops and firemen crowded around the body, elbowing aside the amateur rescuers. Peter watched for a few more minutes, then came over to join her. "Bronwin's dead," he said somberly. "The police have asked us all to stick around for questioning."

Then he realized they were still in their wet evening clothes. "My God, we're soaked! Let's get out of these things before we catch pneumonia."

Carla was totally passive, stunned by her terror of the police. She allowed Peter to lead her back up the stairs. "Does anybody have a coat or something my wife could borrow?" he asked as the passed a knot of guests on the deck. "Her dress is dripping wet."

"She can use mine. I'm warm enough without it." Maud Rucker followed them into the house. She took a baggy black wool coat out of the hallway closet and then led Carla to one of the bathrooms, where she peeled her out of her wet party dress. Carla was shaking violently by this time, mostly from nerves, and Maud had to help her into the coat. The Ruckers were certainly emerging as take-charge types tonight, Carla reflected miserably.

They returned to the living room. Peter had put on his overcoat over his wet suit and he was dripping water onto the white carpet as he argued with Lieutenant Pressner. "If you want to talk to my wife, you'll have to do it right away. Grappling with that dead body in the swimming pool was a traumatic experience. She's obviously in a state of shock, and I want to get her home as quickly as possible."

Pressner grumbled a little, but he gave in when he caught sight of Carla's white face. Little did he suspect that she was suffering from terror. He summoned another cop to join them, then took her elbow and led her down the hall to the empty kitchen.

Carla glanced around the room as he closed the door behind them. The kitchen was decorated in a stagy way with a frieze of china ornaments fastened to the wall above a picture rail, gelatin molds and cookie cutters and novelty plates, and it boasted a restaurant stove and a refrigerator with an ice and drinks dispenser set into the door. Carla didn't recognize any of this, although she knew she must have visited the kitchen earlier in the evening. Where else would she have found a knife that was heavy enough to use to commit murder?

She swallowed, nerving herself to ask for a lawyer. But what lawyer? Who could she call? She didn't know any lawyers in Placer Bar.

Instead, she found herself blurting out a series of questions. "Where was Bronwin stabbed? In what part of her body?" It was very important for her to know. "Have you found the knife yet?"

Pressner gave her a puzzled look. "Where did you get the idea that Mrs. Stauffer was stabbed?"

"Well, I—" Carla clamped her mouth shut just in time. What was she trying to do, confess? she asked herself furiously.

Pressner took a pack of cigarettes from his breast pocket and lit one with a disposable lighter, playing for time as he decided how much to tell her. "She was hit on the back of the head with a rock," he said finally. "It had a happy face painted on the front of it. We found the weapon on the bottom of the pool. The blow may have killed her immediately, or maybe it just knocked her unconscious and her assailant threw her into the water to finish her off. We won't know for sure until after the autopsy."

"A rock?" Carla said stupidly. She was having trouble assimilating the information. There hadn't been any rocks in her reconstruction of the murder.

And a happy face—my God, he was talking about Bronwin's paperweight, that silly rock she used to hold down the magazines on the pool side table. This was unbelievable! She, Carla, must have snatched the damn thing up and slugged her with it.

But at least it didn't sound as if she'd planned the crime. The rock as a weapon seemed to presuppose a quarrel. They'd argued, and then she'd lashed out--

"We're working on the assumption that it was a crime of impulse." Lieutenant Pressner echoed her thoughts. He glanced around and settled himself comfortably on a stool at the kitchen counter. Carla remained standing, stiff inside her borrowed coat. "Somebody followed Mrs. Stauffer when she went out the door, or maybe they made an arrangement to meet. They talked, the conversation became acrimonious—" He shrugged.

"What about bloodstains?" Carla was still trying to explain the lack of blood on her dress.

"There weren't any. Mrs. Stauffer was killed—or stunned, alternatively, if her death was caused by drowning—by a single blow to the head. It didn't break the skin." Pressner's voice rose in irritation. "If the guy had to kill her, I wish he'd hit her a few more times, so she would have bled on him. A bloodstained suspect would make my job a lot easier."

Carla thought it over. "So you're trying to find out who she talked to during the course of the evening, what her movements were."

Pressner nodded. The doctor estimates she's been dead a little more than half an hour, which puts the murder at approximately eight o'clock. That was about fifteen minutes before you went out on the deck and discovered the body."

Fifteen minutes before she found the body? Fifteen whole minutes? Pressner was telling her that she hadn't killed Bronwin! Bronwin had died while she was having that silly run-in with Josie and Pat Graedon, or even back while she was talking with Ned. She wasn't a murderer after all!

Carla's eyes filled with hot tears. Then she broke down entirely, sagging against the counter, her body shaking with great whooping sobs of relief. Through her convulsions, she saw Pressner exchange a look with the other cop. They thought she'd succumbed to hysterics, she realized with the part of her mind that was still functioning. Maybe they weren't so far wrong, at that.

"Look, we just want you to tell us if you saw anybody go out on the deck, either in company with Mrs. Stauffer or immediately before or after the time she left the party. Maybe you saw someone sneaking away through the back yard when you ran down the deck stairs to rescue her?"

Carla shook her head. She was sitting on the floor by now; she vaguely remembered slipping down the face of one of the kitchen cabinets. She'd stopped howling, although the tears still washed down her cheeks in sheets. She gathered the strength to speak. "I didn't even know that Bronwin was out there until I saw her floating in the pool."

"Look, maybe your husband's right. We'll put off questioning you until tomorrow. Can you come down to the station, around ten, say, to give us a formal statement?"

She nodded dumbly and the cops grabbed her elbows and helped her to her feet. She managed to stop weeping as they led her back down the hall to the living room. She collapsed on a couch as they took Peter to the kitchen for a quick round of questions before sending them both home.

She looked up as Maud Rucker handed her a plastic bag. It contained her sodden dress and evening shoes. "Oh, your coat," Carla said dully. "I'll have to return it before we go."

Maud shrugged. "Keep it until tomorrow. Maybe you have a wrap I could use."

The temporary butler produced Carla's evening shawl from the hall closet, a flimsy affair of knitted blue ribbons. Maud admired the garment as she pulled it close around her shoulders. "Not as warm as mine, but a whole lot more stylish."

Peter emerged from the kitchen, still leaving wet footprints as he squished across the white carpet. "Pressner says we can leave now."

They went out to the car. "Poor Owen," he muttered as he held the Nissan's door for her. "This thing has hit him awfully hard. I had a few words with him while you were in the kitchen with the police, and he's half destroyed by grief."

Carla knew she ought to feel pity for Bronwin's husband, but she was numb, drained of all emotion now that she'd been released from her terrible guilt. She wasn't a killer, that was all she could understand. She put her head back against the headrest and closed her eyes, taking refuge in an uneasy exhausted doze as Peter guided the car away from the curb.

Chapter 16

Carla and Peter went down to the police station the next morning to give the cops their formal statements. Carla went first and since they didn't question her intensively, she stuck to the bare facts. She'd gone out on the deck to get some air and she'd lingered there a few minutes before descending the steps to the back yard. She hadn't noticed Bronwin's body right away, but as soon as she did, she'd jumped into the pool. She hadn't had the strength to haul Bronwin out of the water, but she'd managed to push her to the shallow end, where she managed to brace her head up and force some of the water out of her lungs. Then Peter had arrived, followed by the others.

Going back to earlier in the evening, she'd been vaguely aware of people wandering in and out through the glass doors leading to the deck, but no, she couldn't put names to any individuals. She hadn't been paying attention. As far as she was concerned, just about any of the party guests could have joined Bronwin down by the pool.

Pressner took her through her testimony again and again, trying to determine what she'd seen and who she'd talked to from the moment she walked through the Stauffers' front doors. Fortunately for her peace of mind, he seemed more interested in people's movements than in what they'd talked about when they stood together. She told him she'd discussed Owen's building plans with Ned, the changing character of Placer Bar with Pat and Josie, and the Gun Club with Maud Rucker. She left out the fact that everyone she'd talked to had reason to be angry with Bronwin. Pressner seemed resigned to the fact that she could only guess at the times the various encounters had taken place.

It was a tiresome interview, and the surroundings didn't make it any more pleasant. Pressner's office was a linoleum-floored room furnished with a steel desk and plastic chairs, the beige walls decorated with photos of the Lieutenant shaking hands with various local politicos. The only unusual touch was a china figurine on his desk, one of the toys the Japanese used to make shortly after World War II, before they turned their genius to heavy industry, a comic Buddha with a nodding head on a steel spring. The head bobbed every time Pressner's knee touched the desk. Carla's eyes kept returning to the tasteless figurine. For some reason, it annoyed her intensely.

Lieutenant Pressner finally dismissed her, and called Peter into his office to make a statement. Carla could have walked home, but she decided it would be disloyal to leave.

Besides, it was always possible that she might learn something if she hung around the police station. Pressner had refused to answer her questions, explaining that he would be holding a press conference later that afternoon, but maybe she could get somebody else to talk. Carla eyed the cop at the front desk in a speculative way as she took a seat on the long wooden bench in the lobby.

She was in luck. It was the young blond football hero who'd been with the Lieutenant when she discovered the mummified corpse in the linen closet. He owed her one, she told herself. She'd made him very happy by producing that particular dead body, and discovering Bronwin in the swimming pool should have sent her stock even higher.

He finished making an entry in his log book and glanced up. He gave her a sympathetic nod. Evidently he knew why she was here.

She thought it might be best if she could get the cop to initiate the conversation. She let her shoulders slump and gave a loud sigh.

The young man looked a little alarmed, but he didn't say anything. Carla contorted her brow and raised a hand to her mouth as if to hide a spasm of grief.

"Can I get you a glass of water or something, ma'am?" His voice was concerned.

"No, thank you. You're very kind. I'm waiting for my husband, and I don't suppose he'll be long. We came down to give our statements about—oh! About—Bronwin's—murder." Carla let her voice break on the word "murder". She wondered if she were overplaying this.

Evidently not. The young cop leaned forward. "I understand that you're the one who found the body. It must have been a terrible experience."

Good! She'd gotten him to feel sorry for her. Carla launched her attack. "You know the thought that haunts me?" she said in a small voice. "I'm terrified that I may have destroyed some crucial piece of evidence when I tried to pull Bronwin out of the pool. My husband and I tried to rescue her before the police arrived, and I can't help thinking that it may have been a mistake."

"You did the right thing." The cop's face flamed with emotion. "The victim was suffering from concussion, but the doctor gave drowning as the cause of death. You were right to try to save her."

"Oh, God!" Carla cried. "If only I'd been a few minutes earlier!" She wasn't faking this time.

"So it was definitely murder," she went on when she'd recovered herself. "She couldn't have hit her head by accident?"

The cop nodded. "We're acting on the assumption that it was one of her guests at the party."

"But how can you be sure? She was killed in the back yard."

He hesitated for a moment, then succumbed to the urge to gossip. He leaned forward, his blue eyes intent. "You've been to the house. It's on a cul-de-sac at the top of a hill. One of the neighbors was doing a little late gardening that night, and he had his eyes on the Stauffers's house the whole time in question. He would have noticed if anyone had gone around by the side yard instead of entering through the front door."

Carla vaguely remembered the man he was talking about, an elderly fellow wielding a pair of hedge-clippers. He'd given Peter an assessing look when they drove up. She'd wondered at the time if he'd been annoyed because he hadn't been invited to the party, or if he was just worried that one of the guests would try to park in his drive. "What about the back of the house?" she asked abruptly. "The murderer could have crept up the hill."

"The back wasn't so well guarded, but we have a pretty good idea that our murderer didn't come that way." The young cop used his forefinger to sketch a flat-topped hill in the air. "There's a sharp drop-off where the yard ends. The hill falls about two hundred feet down to the access road. We're talking about a 30 degree grade with practically no cover, just a few low bushes and a lot of dried grass. The road was well used that evening with people coming and going from the Stauffers's party, and nobody has reported seeing a suspicious hiker or even a car left where it shouldn't have been. I suppose it's possible the killer could have approached the house without being noticed, but it's highly unlikely. Too many people live in that subdivision."

"What about the guard at the gate of the complex?"

The cop shook his head. "He tells us he only admitted people he was expecting that evening, for what it's worth. Just the residents and their guests—including, of course, the people at the Stauffers's party. He showed us a typewritten list with the names checked off."

"So that narrows things down?"

"Not really. Eighty-three people attended the party, and so far none of them have been able to prove that they couldn't have committed the murder. Not to mention the doorman and the bartender and the five people from the catering service."

"Did you find any blood under Bronwin's fingernails, from defending herself against her attacker? A lost button lying in the grass? Any clues at all?"

He shook his head ruefully. "The victim didn't have a chance to get in any licks of her own, and the murderer was careful. He even wiped the rock for fingerprints before he threw it into the pool."

This was disturbing information. "Good Lord, with ninety suspects, you may never solve this case," she burst out.

The young cop had forgotten all caution by now. "The lieutenant likes the victim's husband for the murderer," he confided.

"Owen?" Carla hated to think that Owen might have done it, but she couldn't very well insist that he hadn't.

"Pressner says the husband is the killer nine times out of ten, and we've heard that they weren't getting along very well. Not only that, several people saw him leave the party at approximately the time the murder must have been committed."

"Sure, I noticed that myself. But Owen went out the front

door!"

The cop shrugged. "He could have doubled back."

"What about the guy with the hedge clippers? He would have seen him."

"The man across the street, you mean? That's a problem. Still, we only have his word for it that he was watching the house the whole time. Surely his attention must have wandered at some point."

"What does Owen say about all this?"

"He has an explanation, all right. He claims the bartender told him he was running out of mixers, and he went to the store to buy some sodas. He was halfway to the shopping center when he remembered that his wife kept a supply of drinks in a second refrigerator down near the pool, so he turned around and came back. He'd rejoined the party and was about to send the bartender out to raid the spare refrigerator when you discovered the body."

"Well, I certainly hope you catch the killer. If only to get poor Owen off the hook."

"We're giving it our best shot, ma'am." The young cop sat up straight and assumed a formal air as Peter and Lieutenant Pressner came into the reception area. They were shaking hands.

"Ready to leave?" Peter took her arm without waiting for an answer. He seemed very pleased with himself as they walked down the street toward their car.

"You know, I've been thinking," he told her as he piloted the Nissan in the direction of their house. "Maybe it's time for me to quit the savings and loan business."

"What?" Carla was astonished. This idea had come out of the clear blue.

"I suppose it's the shock of Bronwin's death. It's kind of

put things into perspective for me. The situation at the office has been getting worse and worse, ever since we moved here. You hate this town, and I'm not so crazy about the place myself. The obvious solution is for me to find another job, one where my boss won't ride me so much. A job where we can move back to San Francisco."

"But—you've been with Cal-Equity for ten years. You're the company's fair-haired boy, the one they've singled out for promotion."

"Not anymore," he said ruefully. "They don't think so much of me now that they're losing money. I don't know if I'll ever recover the ground I've lost this year. They seem to think the recession is my fault. There are easier ways to make a living than managing a failing savings-and-loan office."

"Um," she said thoughtfully, exploring the idea.

"Look at our old friend Jack Dwyer," he went on with rising enthusiasm. "He makes a fortune at that computer sales job of his. He earns a lot more than I do, and it's not as if he has that much on the ball. He's smart, sure, and personable, and I suppose he knows a lot about computers, but I'm mechanically minded and I could learn."

"Of course, Mary contributes to their income," Carla reminded him. "She makes a good salary as chief copywriter for that ad agency."

"I know about computers from a user's point of view. And my job is basically a salesman's. I sell loans instead of mainframes, of course, but I know how to tailor a product to a customer's needs."

"And your experience in banking would be a big plus." Carla was catching fire. "Banks buy computers, lots of them, and with your experience running an office, you'd know exactly what they'd need. Didn't you tell me that Cal-Equity typically pays a couple of hundred thousand dollars for a branch computer system? Not to mention the big machines at headquarters. I'd hire you in a minute if I were a computer company trying to break into the banking market."

"I think I'll give Jack a call, see what he has to say." Peter swung the car into their driveway. "Maybe he can ask around, see if anybody's hiring. And if selling computers doesn't work out, there are plenty of other options to explore."

Knowing Peter and his direct approach to problems, Carla expected him to go straight to the telephone. Instead, he picked up the living room TV and carried it into the bedroom, where he arranged it on the dresser facing the bed. Then he made another trip to the living room for the Sunday paper and the remote control unit.

"Here you go." He plumped up the pillows on the bed invitingly and pulled back the blankets.

"Peter, what are you doing?" she asked, baffled by his behavior.

His face took on a stubborn expression. "That dunking in the pool last night can't have done you any good, and you've had a severe shock. I'm worried about your health in general. You probably don't realize it, but you've been looking awfully pale lately."

"So I'll start wearing more makeup. I'm not sick."

Then Carla realized what he had in mind. Peter wanted her out of the way while he launched his job search. He'd always been a little jealous of the Dwyers and their conspicuously successful lifestyle. They owned a house in Seacliff, one of San Francisco's most exclusive neighborhoods, and it seemed like they were always buying a new Porsche or investing in an antique BMW. Jack and Peter were friends, but there was a competitive aspect to their relationship, and he didn't want her listening in while he asked Jack for a favor.

She took off the dress she'd worn for the police interview and hung it in the closet, then crawled under the covers obediently. He patted her shoulder in approval and handed her the remote control, then went out to the kitchen and closed the door. She heard the clicks of dialing, then the murmur of a low conversation.

She flicked on the TV to give him privacy and hunted through the channels for an interesting program. She circled the dial with the remote before settling on a movie, "Mutiny on the Bounty". The show was half over, but she'd seen it before so she was familiar with the plot. As she remembered it, Marlon Brando's acting was idiosyncratic enough to keep her entertained.

It was probably just as well that Peter had isolated her in the bedroom, she mused, her mind wandering from the action on the screen. He wasn't the only one who wanted to reevaluate what he was doing with his life. She had a few things to think over herself.

She'd fallen into an exhausted slumber the night before, too tired even to brush her teeth, but now the time had come to take stock. She had a nagging feeling at the back of her mind, as if she'd forgotten something vital. Even though she'd proved to her own satisfaction that she wasn't the murderer, she still felt guilty about Bronwin's death. It was the sort of guilt that comes from a neglected responsibility.

And she had good reason to feel that way, she reflected with surprise. She'd been spending a whole lot of time feeling sorry for herself, worrying that the world was treating her badly. But Bronwin was the one who'd really had cause to complain. She, Carla had coveted Bronwin's house, and had been ready to do just about anything to keep her from moving in. Sally had been trying to steal her husband, and Pat Graedon and her supporters were trying to run her out of town.

Not to mention Steve Rucker, who seemed to regard her husband's plans for his factory as an infringement on his personal liberties, or Ned, who'd hated Bronwin because he thought she was out to ruin his contracting career. Half the town had been ranged against the poor woman. They had a lot to answer for, and now had come this final horror. Bronwin had been murdered.

Certainly, Bronwin had been hard to get along with. But who wouldn't have been if they'd been treated that way? Bronwin had fought back bravely, but the town had been too much for her in the end.

Tears sprang to Carla's eyes. She snatched a Kleenex from the bedside table.

She remembered her state of mind when she'd found the body. She'd been under the impression that she was the killer, and of course that hadn't been true—but what about the other element to her thinking, the sense that the murder was connected with the Kettering mansion? Maybe she had something there.

She lay back against the pillows, the movie forgotten and the remote control loose in her hand, and tried to blank out her thoughts, hoping an idea would rise to the surface. Nothing did. But she still had the sensation that she knew something important.

Inspiration had failed her, so she decided to try logic. If her subconscious had a lead to Bronwin's killer, that meant the murderer must be one of her local acquaintances. She reviewed her list of suspects.

There was Owen, for a start. She didn't like it, but she had to admit that Lieutenant Pressner was right. The spouse was the first person to consider when a murder took place, and if the Stauffers's marriage was in trouble, Owen certainly had a financial motive. Bronwin would have made out like a bandit if they'd gotten divorced, and Owen, of course, was in the process of building a new factory. He was probably strapped financially, in need of every last penny, in no position right now to hand over a large chunk of capital to buy his way out of an unhappy marriage. But Carla found it hard to believe that Owen would be ruthless enough to commit murder merely to save a few bucks on alimony. Surely Owen and Bronwin could have struggled on together for another year or two, until the new factory came online. Then he could afford to send her away, lugging her well-filled bags of money to the nearest big city.

Then there was Sally Bolt. No, she told herself, she liked Sally. She didn't want it to be her. But she had to admit that her friend had a motive. She was clearly smitten with Owen, and if what Maud said was true, she was pursuing him fairly aggressively. Maybe Owen was the kind of person who refuses to consider divorce, who considers marriage a binding contract to be honored under all but the most desperate circumstances. Sally might have decided that the only way to get Owen away from his wife was by eliminating Bronwin entirely.

Carla grabbed another tissue and blew her nose angrily. She wasn't going to think about Sally. Let's see now—who in town *didn't* she like? Well, there was Steve Rucker. Maybe he'd killed Bronwin thinking the murder would stop Owen from building his factory, that he'd be so torn up by his wife's death that he'd leave town and never come back. Although, of course, this theory would be more convincing if he'd murdered Owen. That would have put an end to the factory plans for sure. But Owen had been the center of attention at the party, constantly surrounded by a crowd of admiring men. Maybe Steve couldn't get at the electronics entrepreneur, and had settled for killing his wife.

161

Sierra Gothic

Then there was Maud Rucker. Her life revolved around her nephew, from what Carla could gather. Suppose he was threatening to leave town if he lost his "claim" on Casitas Creek. Would she have committed murder to keep him in Placer Bar?

No, she told herself indignantly. The old lady was much too sensible to believe that her nephew had found gold in the river, and she was certainly too sensible to kill for such a foolish reason. And Steve was probably innocent, too. After all, he was the one who'd applied artificial respiration after they pulled Bronwin from the pool.

Or had he been checking to make sure his victim was really dead? Carla had had other things on her mind; she hadn't been watching all that closely. But there had been plenty of onlookers, and surely someone would have noticed if he'd tried something unusual, like choking the woman he was supposedly trying to rescue.

Okay, Carla decided, she'd put the Ruckers aside for a minute. There were other suspects to consider. If the murder had been committed for business reasons, Ned's ambitions looked a lot more compelling than Steve Rucker's delusional dream of finding gold in the creek. Could Ned have killed Bronwin to stop her from telling Owen that he was no good as a contractor? He might have figured he'd have a crack at a job working on the new factory with her out of the way. Or maybe he'd killed her out of spite, to punish her for ruining his chance of earning enough money to build a new house for his family.

She rejected this idea. Ned was her friend. Besides, he was much too level-headed to kill because of a financial disappointment. It wasn't as if his wife and children were going to starve if he lost a job or two.

And if she was going to consider spite as a motive, what about Josie Kettering? She'd run this town for a long, long time,

162

if Maud was to be believed, and Bronwin had made her look like small potatoes. Bronwin was throwing cocktail parties, she'd taken over the Presidency of the Arts Center, and to top it all off, she was restoring the Kettering mansion as a showplace home. Was this a sufficient motive for murder? No, of course not. Josie was pushy, but she wasn't a maniac.

Of course, here again there were two people involved. Howard Kettering, Josie's husband, had seemed pleased about the factory, but perhaps that was just an act. It was perfectly possible that he harbored a violent resentment against the Stauffers, as social and business rivals. Could he have been the killer?

This didn't seem likely. She mentally pictured Howard's round, pleasant face and remembered the cheerful note in his voice as he described Owen's triumphs before the Planning Commission. Surely Howard hadn't killed Bronwin. He was too happy, too content with his life. The murder had been the act of a desperate man.

Or woman. Pat Graedon was the nervous sort, the kind of person who might overreact. She and her husband faced bankruptcy when the factory opened—or they thought they did, which amounted to the same thing. Carla knew from her recent experiences with Peter that business reverses can have a disastrous effect on a person's character, can force them to act in ways they would never have considered previously. Could Pat have killed to save her hotel?

Pat's husband would have had the same motive, but as far as Carla knew, he hadn't been at the party. The young cop at the station had said that Bronwin had been killed by one of her guests, but how could he be sure? The gates at Mother Lode Lodge were manned by a guard, but mainly as a protection against burglars. The guard would question anyone driving a van load of computers and VCRs and TVs out of Mother Lode

Lake, but breaking in was another matter. Nobody patrolled the countryside around the development. There wasn't even a fence. Pat's husband could have hiked in, then waited for a break in traffic to climb the hill to the swimming pool. But how could he have known he'd find Bronwin in her back yard, alone and unprotected, with half the people in town celebrating in the house up above? Pat and her husband would have had to have been in it together. Pat might have sent Bronwin down to the backyard, promising to join her later, and given her waiting husband a signal. Then Pat could have stood sentry in the living room, ready to stop any of the guests who tried to go out on the deck while he was committing the murder.

Too complicated. And way too risky. No sensible person would consider such a scheme for even a minute, and Pat had always struck her as a practical sort. Besides, if she was going to consider a killer coming from the outside, there was no way to prove that the murderer hadn't approached from the front of the house. Surely the watching neighbor, the man with the hedge clippers, had let down his guard at some point during the evening. He wasn't a trained professional hired to keep the Stauffers's house under constant surveillance.

The neighbor could have done it himself. Furious because Bronwin had neglected to invite him to her party, he'd snuck through the back yard and—

Carla shook her head in disgust. She was really reaching here. She jabbed the button on the remote control, jerking up the sound on the TV. She'd be better off watching Marlon Brando than wasting her time on ridiculous speculations.

As if to spite her, a commercial came on and the desperate mutineers were replaced by a man bragging about his dental adhesive. Carla thumbed the sound back down again.

The trouble was, practically everybody she knew had a

motive, but none of the motives seemed convincing. She'd reviewed all the reasons she could think of for killing Bronwin, and she couldn't make herself believe in any of them.

Maybe the police would come up with the answer, although it didn't sound as if they had much to go on. Carla had gathered from Pressner's questions that the cops were trying to build a picture of the evening. They were fitting together people's accounts, looking for a gap or inconsistency. If A was talking to B while X talked to Y, and if O was refilling the punch glasses while P passed the canapes, then Q might have had a chance to slip out unobserved. It must be like putting together an enormous three-dimensional jigsaw puzzle. She wished them luck with the project, but doubted if they'd get far with it. What a headache!

And she couldn't shake the idea that she knew something, that she held the key to the tragedy. Fine, she decided. As soon as Peter let her out of this ridiculous sickbed, she'd look into the problem. She'd talk to all the people in the case on the off-chance that someone would say something that would jog her memory. It couldn't hurt—and it wasn't as if she had anything better to do with her time.

Chapter 17

Carla wasn't the only one with a lot on her mind. Ned called that evening after dinner. "Do you have any idea what we're supposed to do tomorrow? I mean, I haven't actually been fired yet, and under normal circumstances I'd report for work with my crew. But now that Bronwin's been murdered—"

"Good point. She was the one who wanted the house restored; Owen has never been that enthusiastic. One of us ought to get in touch with Owen."

"Are you sure that's a good idea? It seems wrong to intrude on him at this time. I hate to bother the poor guy with our petty personal problems."

Carla thought it over. "We might be making a bigger mistake if we don't. The cops are treating Owen as their main suspect, from what I've heard, and he might think we were avoiding him because we think he's the killer."

"Yeah, I've heard that rumor. Of all the crazy ideas—" His voice trailed off on an indecisive note. Evidently Ned couldn't completely dismiss the possibility that Owen might be guilty.

"We work for the man and we need instructions," she insisted. "It's only normal to ask."

"I still feel uncomfortable. I wouldn't know what to say."

"I'll handle it then. I want to talk to Owen anyway."

"Thanks." Ned sounded very grateful to have this particular task taken off his hands.

Carla broke the connection and dialed Owen's number. As she listened to the phone ring, it occurred to her that the doctor might have Owen under sedation, or he might even be down at the police station answering questions. She was relieved when he picked up the phone.

"This is Carla. I wanted to let you know how shocked and grieved I was by your wife's death." Emotion constricted her throat and she stumbled over the last few words.

"I'm glad you called." Owen's voice was unsteady, but at least he didn't sound groggy from drugs. "You're the first person I've talked to all day apart from the police—and all they wanted to know was whether or not I'd killed my wife." His tone grew weary. "I thought I'd made a few friends in this town, but I guess I was wrong."

"Is there anything I can do to help? I realize that's what people always say at a time like this, but I suppose it fits the circumstances. Have you had anything to eat today?"

"I don't know. I don't think so. I haven't gotten around to fixing a meal, if that's what you mean."

Owen sounded like he was in bad shape. "You shouldn't be alone right now," she told him impulsively. "Why don't I come over? I'll bring you some groceries."

"Sure. Thanks. I'd appreciate that."

Carla knew the delicatessen would be closed by this hour, so she went to the kitchen and raided their refrigerator. She packed a paper bag with bacon and eggs and bread and milk and butter, then added the remains of that night's cauliflower casserole and a package of hamburger from the freezer. Surely the Stauffers had a microwave in that fancy kitchen of theirs that she could use to defrost the meat.

Peter was hard at work in the spare bedroom, updating his

resume. He was more than happy to hand over the car keys. Carla loaded the bag of food in the trunk of the Nissan and set off.

The man who met her at the door was not the self-possessed executive she'd seen at the party, or even the angry homeowner of the night of the fire. Owen carried himself like a confused old man, moving slowly and aimlessly. He paused and looked around a couple of times as he led her to the kitchen, as though he'd forgotten where they were going. Carla wondered if this was due to grief or to sedatives. Perhaps both, she decided.

He rejected her first suggestion, that she fix him a hamburger, so she fried up a dinner of bacon and eggs and toast. Owen sat slumped on a bar stool at the kitchen counter while she worked. It seemed like too much trouble to ask him to move to the dining room so she fed him right there in the kitchen, plunking his plate down on the formica counter. She was starting to feel like a short order cook, so she pulled up another stool and sat down to keep him company while he ate.

"I don't suppose you've had a chance to think about it, but what do you want to do about the Kettering mansion?" She watched him wipe the last scraps of egg from his plate with a piece of toast. "Ned's been wondering whether he should go on with the work."

"I don't want to live in the house, that's for sure. The restoration project was Bronwin's idea." He swallowed a final edge of toast and looked down at his empty plate. "I suppose I'll tell Ned to finish with the new roof, and then I'll put the place on the market."

Carla didn't care what he did with the mansion. The realization dawned on her as a shock. She still felt a certain loyalty to the house, and she was glad that Owen wasn't going to leave the roof open to the wind and rain, but he could sell it to a stranger tomorrow as far as she was concerned. It had taken Bronwin's death to free her, but the house had been exorcised from her life at last.

She lowered her head and swabbed at the counter with a paper napkin to hide her intense relief. "I'll tell Ned to report for work as usual, then," she mumbled. "I guess my job is finished, though. You won't need my help if you've given up on the idea of doing a historically accurate restoration."

Owen turned to face her at that last remark, and he looked her in the eye for the first time. He seemed troubled; she realized that he didn't like the idea of firing her. She put up a hand to forestall any objections. "I was almost through, anyway."

She poured herself a cup of coffee. She still had Owen to worry about. "The next question is, what are your personal plans? Are you going to move back to Sacramento?"

"Sacramento?" He seemed surprised at the question. "I can't go back there, not with the factory coming to town."

"You're still moving the factory to Placer Bar?" Carla had somehow assumed that Bronwin's death would put a stop to that project.

"I don't have any choice, not at this point. We've bought the land and now I'm committed to the move."

"But you're the president of the company. Can't you change your mind?"

"I don't run the business to suit myself. We issued stock a few years back, and now I have to answer to the shareholders. Canceling the move would cost a ton of money. My Board of Directors would never go along." He pondered what she'd said. "You're right, though. I do need a change. I don't want to stay on in this house now that Bronwin is dead."

"Maybe you should check into the Miner's Palace Hotel, for the time being, at least," Carla suggested. Then she remembered that Pat Graedon, and presumably her husband, were Owen's sworn enemies. Well, that didn't matter. They could hardly refuse to give him shelter under the circumstances.

Owen's face brightened. He seemed to like the idea of moving to the hotel. "That might be my best bet."

She followed him to the master bedroom and watched as he began throwing socks into a suitcase. He'd packed almost a full drawer of them before he realized what he was doing.

"I sure do have a lot of socks." He dumped them out on the bed and went to the closet. Paying more attention this time, he chose several suits and some casual pants and shirts. Carla collected his toiletries from the connecting bathroom while he folded his clothes into the suitcase.

She was beginning to feel responsible for Owen, and she insisted on following him in her car to the Miner's Palace. If Pat caused any difficulties, she'd invite Owen to stay with her and Peter.

Besides, Pat was on her list of suspects. It might be illuminating to see her reaction when she learned that Bronwin's death wasn't going to stop the factory from coming to Placer Bar.

Pat was working the check-in desk, and she was visibly taken aback when the two of them straggled into the hotel lobby. She recovered quickly, though, and handed Owen the key to her best room with a look of genuine sympathy. Carla was glad to see that Pat didn't let her financial interests stop her from coming to Owen's help in his time of trouble.

Owen said he could manage his suitcase, and Pat directed him up the stairs to his temporary quarters. "Can I buy you a drink?" Carla asked the hotel keeper. "I'd like to have a word."

Pat started to shake her head, then changed her mind. "Yeah, that would be nice. I don't suppose we'll get any more guests this evening. It's almost ten. We'll have to sit where I can keep an eye on the lobby, though."

The hotel bar was fairly busy considering that it was a Sunday night. The hotel had attracted the end-of-summer tourist trade, Carla supposed. "It's good to get off my feet," Pat confided as they slipped into a booth. "There's always some job that needs doing when you own a hotel, and most of them involve walking and carrying heavy objects. It's almost as bad as being a waitress. Now, what was it you wanted to talk about?"

"I don't know how to put this. Well, to be blunt, does it bother you having Owen here? I know how you feel about the factory, and I thought I ought to let you know that Bronwin's death isn't going to change his plans. He says it's too late to back out, now that he's bought the land."

Pat's face turned pale. "I'd hoped—but I suppose it was too much to ask," she murmured.

"I could ask him to stay at our house. I haven't had a chance to talk to my husband, but I'm sure he wouldn't mind."

Pat waved aside this suggestion. "Oh, I have nothing against Owen personally. I feel sorry for him, losing his wife that way. And we can use the business. With the factory coming to town, we'll need every dollar we can earn."

Pat's voice was strained, but Carla decided to take her words at face value. "Good. I was afraid that it might be awkward for you, literally sheltering the enemy under your own roof."

The waitress came over. Carla asked for a beer and Pat told her to bring two of them. "One project Owen *has* given up on is restoring the Kettering mansion. He says he's going to put the house on the market once the roof is fixed."

Pat's gaze shifted to the middle distance and she caught her lower lip with her teeth. "Hmmm. That place would make a wonderful bed-and-breakfast. That pillared facade would attract the tourists like flies to honey. But what am I thinking of? Owen is going to ruin the town for vacationers looking for a romantic getaway." She shook her head, dismissing the thought.

Carla sat up straight, struck by a new thought. "You know what would be wonderful? If the Kettering mansion could be used for some community purpose. Maybe the town could buy it and turn it into a museum or a meeting hall. I'll bet Owen would sell it to them cheap."

Fired up with enthusiasm, she leaned across the table. "Pat, you seem to be good at organizing things. I know you didn't have much luck with your petition to keep big industry out of Placer Bar, but promoting the Kettering mansion would be different. We're talking about creating more jobs *and* attracting more tourists." Carla had completely sold herself on the idea of opening the mansion to the public.

The waitress came back and slid their drinks in front of them. Pat stared into her beer with lackluster eyes. "Oh, God," she sighed. "I don't have the strength for another battle.

"You don't know what it's been like," she continued, her voice increasing in volume. "The struggle to buy this hotel, then begging the bank for money to fix it up. My husband and I spent every weekend haunting auctions and antique shops looking for furniture we could afford. Now the cooks and the waitresses and the bartenders keep quitting. Our suppliers don't show up, or if they do, they try to sell us second-rate goods. Just keeping this damn hotel in business is a seven day a week operation, and I'm talking about fifteen-hour days.

"Then on top of that, there's all the political stuff. Hassles with the Planning Commission every time we want to pound a nail into one of our historically significant walls. Pressuring the Chamber of Commerce to host more events to attract the tourists. I let them talk me into serving on the Pioneer Days committee, and you wouldn't believe the headache that's been. I lived in England for a while, back when my husband and I roamed the world working in other people's hotels. I can tell you, these small-town California festivals are even more cut-throat than an English church fete. The Boy Scouts and the Rotary aren't speaking to each other; they're squabbling over who's going to get the prime booth location on Main Street, the one that's closest to the freeway. The Downtown Merchants and the Mother Lode Lake Homeowners *both* came up with the idea of selling teriyaki, and neither group is willing to back down. They still haven't reached a compromise and Pioneer Days starts this very weekend. Just how much Japanese barbecue do they think they can sell?

"And now you want me to start a movement to turn the Kettering mansion into some kind of public meeting place? It's a worthwhile cause, but count me out. That wouldn't be the straw that broke the camel's back. It would be a whole big bag of cement!"

A hysterical note had infected Pat's voice during the last part of her tirade, but now she sat back in her chair, a dreamy look on her face. "You know what I wish I could do? I'd like to rent an apartment in a shiny new apartment block and get a salaried job with a large corporation. Then I could go to work every day at a regular hour, and when I came home, I'd have my evenings and weekends all to myself."

"I'm sorry—" Carla stammered.

"Oh, I don't mean it. Of course not." Pat gave her shoulders a little shake. "It's just that there are so many problems with your plan. The city isn't going to buy the Kettering mansion. Placer Bar doesn't have the money. Tax collections are way down, what with all the unemployment we have now, and the Mayor just spent his entire development budget on reopening the Ebbets Mine."

"Yes, I heard about that," Carla cried, relieved at the change in subject. "The old gold mine that runs right under Broad Street. They're fixing it up and opening it to the public. It's supposed to be the highlight of the Pioneer Days festival."

"This whole town is built on top of a system of mine tunnels. The miners figured, why commute to work? The Ebbets mine is only one of many. They've shored the walls up and installed a system of electrified mine carts to carry the people down. It ought to attract a lot of visitors. The Mayor will hold the ribbon-cutting ceremony on Tuesday, so we locals can see what they've done before the festival opens and the mine fills up with tourists."

The waitress arrived with two new beers at this point and Carla handed her a twenty.

"I'm sorry I snapped at you." Pat looked a little abashed. "Actually, you're right. It would be nice if we could find a good use for the Kettering mansion."

"If the city is out as a purchaser, what about a private group? The Historical Society, for instance. Their library is awfully cramped. Or the Arts Center."

Pat pursed her lips doubtfully. "They're both broke, too." Then she snapped her fingers. "I've got it! The Clampers! They've been looking for a place to establish a Gold Rush museum."

"The what?"

"E Clampus Vitus. My husband, Lucas, is the Grand Noble Humbug of the local chapter." There was unmistakable pride in Pat's voice as she made this unlikely statement.

"Grand Humbug?" Carla was beginning to wonder just how seriously Pat had been affected by overwork.

"E Clampus Vitus is an organization dedicated to preserving the memory of the Gold Rush days," Pat explained. "They study local history and collect records and put up monuments, that sort of thing. They do a lot of drinking, too. In fact, they spend a lot of time debating as to whether they're a drinking historical society or a historical drinking society."

Carla was a little confused by the turn the conversation had taken, but at least Pat seemed to be on the right track. The two of them would find a good use for the mansion yet. "Maybe I ought to join the Clampers," she offered. "My husband keeps encouraging me to participate more in civic activities."

Pat glanced down in embarrassment. "They don't have any women members. At least, I don't know of any. It's basically a drinking club; the men get together to laugh and cut up."

"I didn't realize it was a men's lodge." Carla took a swig of her beer. "What does the name mean," she added sourly. "'No Girls Allowed?'"

"It doesn't mean anything. E Clampus Vitus is just a string of Latin-sounding syllables." Pat had recovered from her moment of awkwardness. "The Clampers aren't exactly a lodge, either. It's hard to describe them."

She ran a finger around the edge of her beer glass, marshaling her thoughts. "Back in the nineteenth century, a lot of people belonged to fraternal orders like the Masons and the Odd Fellows. The groups were mainly social clubs, but they also took care of their members when they got in trouble. Today we have Welfare, and most people get health benefits through their jobs, but back then a wife and children could starve if the breadwinner died or became disabled. The lodges raised money to support these families. Even then they were considered a bit laughable, though, with their initiation rites and secret handshakes. A group of California miners started E Clampus Vitus as a spoof on the other groups. The way it worked back in the 1850's, everyone in these small mining towns would pretend that E Clampus was a regular lodge. They'd talk newcomers into joining by convincing them they had to if they wanted to do business in the area. After the new member had been put through a thoroughly silly ceremony, they'd spend his initiation fee on booze and hold a huge drinking party. At that point the new guy would realize that he'd been tricked, and the only way he could get his own back was to find another victim. The system was self-perpetuating."

"What a strange idea. Still, I suppose it was an efficient way to finance drunken brawls."

"It's a little more formal these days. People usually know what they're letting themselves in for when they join. They keep up a lot of the old traditions, though. For example, all the members are officers, with titles like 'Imperturbable Hangman' or 'Damfool Doorkeepers'. They like to say that all their offices are of equal indignity."

"I can see why they don't want women members. Men like to think they have a monopoly on silly jokes."

"Oh, there's more to it than that. My husband is working on a Civil War memorial right now."

"The Civil War? In Placer Bar?" This small mountain town certainly seemed determined to involve itself in the nation's conflicts, Carla told herself, remembering the Gray Ladies and their World War II attack on City Hall.

"Oh, we were far away from the action, of course, but feelings ran high. A lot of men went back East to fight or help their families. Lucas's first idea was to put up a monument to the local soldiers who served in the war, on both sides. But the records were incomplete and he would have left some names off, which wouldn't have been fair. They finally decided to raise a memorial to the 'Great Scare' of 1865."

Carla raised her eyebrows and Pat went on to explain.

"Most of the people in Placer Bar were Union supporters, including the newspaper editor at that time, but there were a number of Southerners on the outlying ranches. One day a rumor hit town that the Confederate sympathizers were tired of all the talk about preserving the Union and they planned to ride into town and beat the shit out of any Yankees they could get their hands on. The Sheriff and the editor and a lot of the other leading citizens panicked and ran for the hills. They didn't come back for three days, when someone finally sent them word that the Southerners' attack hadn't materialized."

Carla decided she liked the idea of a war memorial dedicated to a bunch of cowardly civilians. "I can see the Clampers work hard to preserve the glorious history of the region."

A short, plump man with a weather-beaten outdoor complexion and a lush brown beard walked into the bar. He looked aggressively Western in a red-and-black checked lumberjack shirt, blue jeans and engineer's boots. He glanced around, spotted Pat, and came over to their table. He kissed her cheek and pulled up an empty chair. "Taking a break, hon?"

"Carla, this is Lucas, my husband. Lucas, Carla Weber." Then Pat's voice changed, growing intimate. "I was just telling Carla about the Civil War memorial."

"Like to see an artist's drawing?" Without waiting for Carla to reply, Lucas reached into his back jeans pocket and produced a worn wallet. He unfolded a sheet of paper and handed it to her. "We thought we'd put up a marble obelisque about five feet high with a brass plaque on the front."

Carla glanced at the sheet of paper. The drawing showed a squat version of the Washington Monument. The plaque on it read, "Civil War, 1861-1865", and under it the words "Honoring the Great Scare". The text describing the incident evidently hadn't been worked out yet, since the body of the plaque was represented by squiggles.

"We're going to put the monument in the little park at the corner of Broad and Beal, near the entrance to the Ebbets Mine. We were hoping to be able to hold the unveiling at the mine opening ceremony, but we haven't managed to get the damn thing carved yet. We Clampers have a little trouble getting organized at times." Lucas retrieved the drawing from Carla and slipped it back into his wallet.

"Very nice," she told him.

"You're Peter Weber's wife, aren't you?" Carla nodded and he gave her a wink. "Tell your husband that if he plays his cards right, we might consider putting a plaque on his trailer honoring it as the first savings and loan office in Placer Bar.

"Of course," he went on, rubbing his beard thoughtfully, "it would help if he eloped with a beautiful teller and the contents of the vault. We like to celebrate events of genuine historical importance."

Carla started to giggle, then checked herself. "I wouldn't say that to Peter, if I were you. He's sensitive these days when it comes to his business."

"A stuffy banker, huh? I know the type. I'll be careful of his feelings. I might want to borrow money from him one of these days."

There was nothing Carla could put her finger on, but Pat and Lucas Graedon had assumed the air that couples take on when they have something to discuss in private. She rose to her feet. "It's been nice talking to you. And Pat—think over what I said about the Kettering mansion. I'll be in touch."

She hadn't actually learned very much that evening, she reflected as she headed for the hotel parking lot and Peter's car. Owen seemed genuinely broken up by his wife's death, but she couldn't scratch him as a suspect. He could have killed Bronwin and then realized too late that he didn't have the emotional distance necessary to commit a murder.

She liked Pat Graedon now that she'd gotten to know her a little better, and Lucas had a certain rough charm, but she couldn't rule them out, either. If anything, she'd discovered that the couple was under a tremendous amount of financial pressure, even more than she'd realized.

Well, she had other people to talk to. She resolved to suspend judgment until she'd talked to the rest of her suspects.

Chapter 18

Peter was asleep when Carla got home that night, and he seemed in a distracted mood at breakfast. She told him about her conversation with Owen, thinking he'd be pleased to learn that the new factory would still be coming to Placer Bar, but he greeted the news with an indifferent shrug. He seemed to have lost all interest in the future of his savings and loan office. His attention was focused on finding a new job.

"Jack said he'd try to set up a few interviews with people in his company," he confided as he bolted his second cup of coffee. "They aren't actually looking for a new sales rep, but sometimes they'll create a position if the right person comes along."

"I hope it works out for you."

"If it doesn't, there are other places I can try for a job." He glanced at his watch. "I suppose I should make an effort to be on time for work today. I'll be taking enough time off for job-hunting trips to San Francisco over the next few weeks." He gave her a quick kiss and headed out the door.

Left on her own, Carla stared thoughtfully out the window. The next item on her agenda was to visit Sally Bolt and see what she had to say about Bronwin's murder, but she wasn't anxious to put this plan into operation. She was fond of Sally and the thought of pumping her for information was faintly repulsive. And if Sally really was in love with Owen, if there was more going on than a harmless flirtation, the conversation was bound to be awkward in the extreme. How did you go about asking a woman if she'd murdered her lover's wife?

Not that she believed Sally was guilty, of course. She told herself that Sally was a real standout, with her long black hair and vivid eye makeup. People would remember her movements on the night of the party. The police might even have put together an alibi for her by now, patching together the recollections of the other guests. Comforting herself with this thought, she washed the breakfast dishes and set off for Sally's house.

Sally wasn't pleased to find Carla on her doorstep. In fact, she seemed downright hostile. She opened the door a few inches and peered out with a "show me why I should bother" expression. Her face was drawn and pale; it looked like she hadn't slept well since the night of Bronwin's murder. "Yes?" she demanded, as if Carla was a canvasser trying to sell magazines.

"I hate to trouble you, but we've got to do something about Owen," Carla blurted out. "The poor man desperately needs a friend right now."

Sally flinched at the mention of Owen's name, and her eyes narrowed. Carla thought she was going to ask her to leave, but then Sally changed her mind. She stepped back from the door, giving Carla a wary look. "You'd better come in."

This was going to be rougher than she realized. She hadn't asked any questions, and Sally was already treating her like an opponent. Carla followed her friend to the kitchen. Sally waved her to a chair at the circular pine table and went to the stove to make a fresh pot of coffee.

"What's this about Owen?" Sally's voice was level and her back was turned so Carla couldn't read her expression.

"Bronwin's murder has hit him hard. He's in terrible shape emotionally and he needs support. You know how it is when there's a death in the family. Your friends and neighbors come by with food and offers of help. Well, I talked to Owen yesterday—in fact, I went over to his house and helped him move into the Miner's Palace Hotel. He said nobody in town has even bothered to call him since the night of the party. Except for the cops, of course, and they've been treating him as their principal suspect."

The water came to a spitting boil and Sally emptied the kettle into the Melitta's ceramic funnel. She carried the pot over to the table and sat down heavily. She poured out two cups of coffee and shoved one of them in Carla's direction without a word. Unnerved by her silence, Carla continued to chatter away.

"I can understand, of course. Owen hasn't lived in town for very long and none of us know him well enough to feel comfortable approaching him. As Ned Fielding said yesterday, we don't want to intrude on his grief. But the poor guy is awfully isolated right now. I just thought—" She screwed up her mouth and spread her hands in a helpless gesture.

"Okay. I'll send him some flowers. If he's staying at the Miner's Palace he won't be able to use a casserole, since he'll be eating his meals in the restaurant." Sally's eyes were hard and black, like shiny river rocks.

Carla didn't know what she'd been expecting, but it hadn't been this. Sally was behaving as if Owen were a charity she didn't particularly approve of, and Carla had pressured her into making a donation. Carla took a quick gulp of coffee to cover her confusion, burning her mouth in her haste.

Sally ignored her gasp of pain. "Just why did you come to me with this problem?" Carla detected a note of emotion in her voice at last. She didn't wait for a reply. "I suppose you've heard the rumors about the way Owen and I have been carrying on."

Carla was flummoxed. "Ah. Oh. Well, Maud did say something the other day about the two of you sharing a target at the Gun Club." Carla figured there was no use denying that she'd heard about the scandal.

Sally stared at her blankly for a moment and then the hard look faded from her face. "The rumors are true."

Sally burst into tears. Overwhelmed by a rush of sympathy, Carla grabbed a paper napkin from the rack on the table and pushed it into her friend's hand.

Sally didn't weep for very long, but her eyes were haunted as she looked up and appealed to Carla for understanding. "I think I've been in love with Owen ever since we met, three years ago. It didn't really matter while my husband was still alive. I was happy with my marriage and it was only a game, flirting with Owen when he came up here for the hunting season, dreaming about the way it might have been. We both felt a strong attraction, but we assumed it would never lead to anything. But now I'm single, and that makes all the difference. I tried to avoid him when he first came to town, but then I heard that his marriage was in trouble. I thought, okay, if he's going to leave his wife anyway, why shouldn't I take advantage of the situation? He'll need someone new, and why shouldn't it be me? So I started going down to the Gun Club, where I knew I'd run into him."

Carla remembered the yellow corduroy jacket she'd noticed on Sally's coat rack the day she'd first visited her house. Owen had been wearing that jacket on the night of the fire. It looked as if Maud was right—the two of them had been seriously involved for some time.

She gazed at Sally, feeling perplexed. "I don't get it. Owen's lonely, he's in trouble, he needs a friend, and you love him. Why aren't you over at the Miner's Palace right now?"

"It isn't that simple. Have you ever had a husband drop dead on you?"

The question was obviously rhetorical and Sally went on without waiting for a reply. "When Chuck died, I couldn't believe it at first. I'd wake up every morning and my heart would leap with hope; I'd tell myself it wasn't true. Then I'd realize that the bed was empty, but I still couldn't fully accept that he was gone. Every time the phone rang, my first thought would be that it was Chuck on the line, calling to tell me there'd been some terrible mistake."

Her lips tightened into a thin line. "Those were the easy days. Then it finally sunk in that Chuck was truly dead. I went into a deep depression. I was sure my life was over."

Carla leaned forward, longing to be of comfort. "But Owen doesn't have to go through that. Not the way you did, anyway. You can help him. He loves you, you love him—you should be at his side."

Sally's face contracted with pain again. "That's easy for you to say. I just don't know what to do. My first impulse was to tell him we should be together. But then I lost my nerve. His marriage wasn't very successful, and he and Bronwin would have broken up eventually, I'm sure, but that doesn't mean he didn't care about her. He has a lot of grieving to go through. I wouldn't want him to think I was trying to take advantage of his loss. That might turn him against me. Besides, there's a lot of sense to the rule that people should wait a few months before getting emotionally involved again, after someone they loved has died. I was a real wreck when Chuck was killed in that accident, and it would have been a big mistake if I'd taken up with another man right away. I wasn't in any shape for a new love affair."

"But surely Owen's case is different."

"It just wouldn't feel right to offer to take Bronwin's place. Not now, anyway. I felt bad enough about my behavior when she was still alive. Running around with another woman's husband is a lousy thing to do. But Bronwin seemed so strong, so self-assured. I told myself that if she really wanted Owen, it was up to her to keep him." Sally laughed mirthlessly. "I know I'm being irrational. I didn't worry about Bronwin's feelings when she was alive. Now that she's dead and I can't possibly hurt her, I'm consumed with guilt."

Carla could understand that. "Why don't you write Owen a letter? You know, just an ordinary condolence note, the sort of thing that anyone might write."

"It's an idea," Sally said slowly. "Owen would see that I was offering to be there for him if he needed me."

"I think you should do it. Owen's hurting too, and you've got to think of him." Carla paused, not sure if it was the right thing to say, then decided to go ahead. "Maud Rucker thinks you make a nice couple."

Sally looked embarrassed. She was probably having second thoughts about confiding her troubles in someone she didn't know very well. She hastened to change the subject. "It's a funny thing about the Ruckers. They've been acting very strangely lately, both Steve and Maud. A friend of mine ran into Steve last week at a Sacramento car dealership. He was looking at expensive four-wheel-drive trucks and talking as if he planned to buy one. Then I saw Maud at the supermarket the other day. She had beans in her shopping cart, but she said things would be looking up for them soon. She kept dropping hints to the effect that the Kettering mansion wasn't the only old building in town scheduled for restoration. She must have been referring to her own house."

Carla agreed that Sally's information was intriguing. "The

185

Ruckers can't afford a new car, much less a big contracting job. Do you think that Maud's deluding herself—or is Steve tricking her in some way?"

"I don't know. I've always thought of Maud as a sharp old lady. I'd hate to think that her mind was going."

Carla hated to think of the alternative, that the Ruckers might actually be coming into a large sum of money. She remembered her suspicion that Steve was planning to blackmail Owen. She was going to have to talk to Maud and see if she could discover the source of their anticipated wealth.

"I'd better leave you to write your letter," she said, getting up from the table. Sally showed her to the door.

What pretext could she use to visit the Ruckers? Carla remembered the black coat she'd borrowed from Maud. She should have returned it the day before. She hurried home and collected the garment, and on her way back down Broad Street she stopped at the village bakery and bought a banana cake as well. If she arrived with a dessert in hand, Maud would have to invite her in to eat some.

Maud and her nephew were working at the back of the house when she got there, clearing away blackberry vines that had grown into a high tangle over most of the yard. Steve was uprooting the bushes with a mattock, a primitive-looking combination pick and hoe. Maud, her hands protected by heavy leather gloves, was packing the vines into cardboard boxes so they could be hauled to the dump.

"You never come empty-handed," Maud said when Carla handed her the cake. "I'll fix us something to drink with this." She went through the back door into the kitchen, leaving Steve and Carla alone in the small part of the yard that hadn't been taken over by the blackberries.

"We'll be in a position soon to repay your kindness." Steve's voice was gruff, with an undertone of resentment.

Maud came out again before Carla could reply. She was carrying a tray with three tumblers of lemonade and three chipped china plates with hand-painted butterflies decorating the rims. The plates would have been valuable if they'd been perfect, Carla reflected. Even flawed, they were charming. The three of them sat down on the rickety back steps to enjoy their treat.

"Have you heard? Owen's checked into the Miner's Palace Hotel." Carla kept her tone light and gossipy, pretending that she only wanted to share the latest news. "He said he couldn't bear to go on living at their house at Mother Lode Lake."

"I feel so sorry for him. I don't think their marriage was in very good shape, but that's a terrible way to lose a wife." Maud cut thick slices of the cake and handed the plates around.

"He's given up on his plans for the Kettering mansion, but he still intends to move the factory here. I suppose he'll be looking for a new place to live."

Maud wielded her fork busily. "I'm glad to hear it about the factory. This town desperately needs jobs."

"Just as long as he doesn't build his damn factory on my claim." Steve had finished his cake in double-quick time. He rose to his feet, handing the empty plate to his aunt.

"Yes, of course, dear," she said absently. "I'm sure he'll find another site."

"I'll be back in an hour or so." Steve waved to his aunt and left them, walking quickly around the side of the house.

Maud seemed a little surprised at his sudden departure, but Carla had been expecting something of the sort. Steve Rucker was definitely trying to avoid her.

She followed Maud into the kitchen and glanced around the room as her hostess rinsed the plates. A glossy catalog lying on the cracked linoleum counter caught her eye. She picked it up. It came from a firm specializing in antique and discontinued china and silverware patterns. The company claimed to be able to supply pieces for almost any set, but their prices struck her as awfully high.

"What's this?" she asked. "You're thinking of buying new dishes?"

"Used ones, actually. They get most of their stock from estate sales, that sort of thing.

"My old china service is in sorry shape," Maud went on, holding up one of the cracked plates and examining it critically. "I only have a few pieces left. Steve offered to buy me a new set, any pattern I like, but I've always been fond of this one. He spoils me. He talked to an antique dealer and the man put me in touch with the catalog firm."

Carla couldn't think of a tactful way to put it. She decided to be blunt. "Steve's going to pay for this with gold from Casitas Creek?"

Maud didn't answer. Her eyes gleamed with fun, though, and Carla realized that the old lady was having her on. But she was probably serious about the money, whether she was deluding herself or not, Carla told herself. Maud was not the type to send off for a catalog just to indulge in a consumer fantasy.

A shadow crossed Maud's face. "Of course, Steve will want to get his own place once he makes his pile. I don't blame him, he needs his independence, but I'll miss having him around the house."

"He'll be staying on in Placer Bar, then?"

Maud nodded emphatically.

"To work his claim?"

Maud ignored the question. "I'm glad that Owen's made up his mind to stay here, too. This town hasn't treated him kindly, but he's a young man yet. He'll recover, and go on to build a good life for himself."

"Unless he's arrested for Bronwin's murder," Carla said somberly. "The police have been questioning him at length. You don't suppose he did it, do you?"

Carla had thrown the question out at random, hoping for a revealing response. Maud's answer surprised her. She wiped the last plate dry and put it in the cupboard, then pursed her lips and looked her straight in the eye. "I don't know, and I don't suppose we'll ever find out. Owen's a smart fellow, and if he's the murderer I expect he'll have covered his tracks."

Carla was shocked. "Don't you care about justice?"

"Not really, no. Oh, if I thought Owen was some kind of mad killer and was likely to start running around bludgeoning people wholesale, I'd want to see him stopped. But it isn't that kind of situation. If Owen killed his wife, he probably had a good reason for doing it, and he's not likely to try anything like that again. I never cared about Bronwin and I'm not close enough to the situation to feel strongly about seeing her murderer brought to book."

Maud took off her apron and hung it on a nail in the wall, then began herding Carla towards the front door. She was amiable enough about this, but it was clear that she was ready for her guest to leave. "It was nice of you to come by and bring us the news," she said as she urged her down the hall. "Drop by anytime." She opened the door and practically pushed her out onto the porch.

"Hey! My shawl!" Carla cried.

Maud shook her head in self-reproach, then ducked back into the house and produced the garment from the hall closet. She stroked the silky material before handing it over. "Maybe I'll ask Steve to buy me one of these." Her lips curved in a pleased smile.

Carla was thoroughly confused as she set off down the

sidewalk. Her inquiries were getting her nowhere. All she'd learned today was that Sally had had a strong motive for getting rid of Bronwin, and that Maud took a remarkably casual attitude towards violent crime. It didn't seem credible that either of them was the murderer, but she couldn't rule them out.

The one thing that was clear to her was that she didn't feel like going home. She decided to treat herself to lunch at the Miner's Palace Hotel. Maybe she would run into Owen. And even if she didn't she'd be sure to pick up some new gossip. The hotel bar was the town's central rumors exchange.

Chapter 19

Carla had often wondered why Placer Bar's downtown area was so extensive, but as she picked her way along a wooden sidewalk she remembered what Sally had said about the old days. The town had been the urban center for a large floating population of miners, trappers and other fortune seekers who'd scratched out a living in the surrounding wilderness. The little town had been important once, big enough to need more than one street of shops and saloons.

Most of the buildings were nothing more than poorly constructed tin-roofed shacks behind their brave false fronts, but the Miner's Palace Hotel was one of the exceptions. It was a brick building, five stories high, with delicate, somewhat dangerous-looking wrought-iron balconies decorating the front windows of the guest rooms.

Carla had almost reached the door to the restaurant when she encountered Josie Kettering. Josie was coming out of the dry goods store and she was in quite a state. Her lips were trembling and her face was screwed up in misery. She looked like she was about to burst into tears.

"What's wrong?" Carla asked, putting a hand on Josie's arm.

"Those idiots still don't have my special plant food," Josie wailed. "I ordered it three months ago and they haven't gotten it in yet. What a way to run a business! If my husband's bank operated like that, we'd have closed down years ago."

Carla knew that Josie was a dedicated gardener, but her reaction to the plant food crisis seemed a little extreme. "Can't you get the stuff somewhere else? I think there's a nursery on the edge of town."

"No, I can't! It's a special type of fertilizer, powdered fish meal. I read about it in a rose book. Nobody around here carries it, that's why I had to place a special order. They say there's a strike at the factory and they don't know when they'll get it in—but what am I supposed to do in the meantime? My roses need it now if I'm going to win first prize at the County Fair."

Carla was beginning to understand why Josie was so upset. It had been a bitter blow when Bronwin took over as President of the Arts Center. Josie had diverted her ambitions to the flower show, but now her efforts in that direction had been frustrated, too.

"I have an idea. I never gave you those trout I promised at your tea party. Do you think they'd do as well as the commercial ground fish?"

Josie's expression grew a little less miserable. "It's worth a try. Tell you what—why don't you bring the trout by my house in about an hour? I'll show you my roses and fix us something to eat."

Abandoning her plan to have lunch at the hotel, Carla went home to collect the remaining trout in her freezer. She certainly wasn't living the life of a recluse anymore, she reflected ruefully as she packed the fish in a cardboard box. Between her work on the restoration project and looking into Bronwin's death, she'd become thoroughly embroiled in the life of the town.

"Leave the fish in the kitchen," Josie directed when Carla reached her house. "I want to show you my garden."

Carla was glad to put the heavy box on a counter. They went out the back door. Josie's lawn was a vivid green, unblemished by weeds, and the rich plush texture of the grass made Carla wonder if Josie used a roller on it.

Beds of flowers blazed in the noonday sun. Carla recognized some old favorites—snapdragons, wallflowers, tiny pansies—but many of the species were unfamiliar. Josie recited their Latin names, affectionate pride in her voice. When she realized that the technical terms meant nothing to her guest, she stopped talking and let Carla drink in the glorious colors.

Most of the roses were in a carefully weeded bed at the foot of the garden. The plants seemed in remarkably healthy condition, with deep green glossy leaves and perfectly formed flowers and buds. Josie flushed with pleasure when Carla exclaimed over a bush of crimson flowers.

As they walked back to the house, Carla reflected that she had seen Josie's soul. People are shaped by their passions, and Josie's love was her garden. The dumpy, pretentious matron no longer seemed like a figure of fun.

They found Howard Kettering waiting for them in the kitchen. He'd come home for lunch.

"Fish! An unexpected treat." He rubbed his hands together with pleasure as he peered into the cardboard box. "Where'd we get all the trout?"

"Those are for the garden," Josie told him. She slapped his arm playfully. "We're having some sandwiches I picked up at the delicatessen."

Howard's face fell. Carla suspected that he was as sick of takeout food as Peter was. Of course, Peter was also sick of fish.

Josie opened her refrigerator and produced three film-wrapped sandwiches on paper plates. "Grab a few cans of soft drinks, will you?" she said to Carla, holding the refrigerator door open with her knee. "Howard, could you get the silverware and napkins?"

The side pockets of the refrigerator held the expected selection of condiments, and the top shelf was evidently kept free for snacks from the deli, but the central shelf had been taken out to make room for a couple of large paper grocery sacks. "Drinks?" Carla said, looking at the bags, confused as to proceed.

"I think you'll find some Cokes in that sack on the left."

Carla took the bag out of the refrigerator. She set it next to the carton of fish and peeked inside. An economy sized package of toilet paper rested on top of a whole chicken and a box of detergent.

"Why do you keep your toilet paper in the refrigerator?" she asked, fascinated by this new approach to domestic life.

"Saves time." Josie seemed proud of herself. "When I come home from the grocery store I just pop the bags in the refrigerator. The perishable stuff stays cold, and of course it can't hurt the other things." She pushed through a swinging door into the dining room.

Carla couldn't very well argue with this. She rooted around until she found three Cokes at the bottom of the bag and followed Josie into the dining room. The paper plates and plastic tubs of coleslaw looked incongruously picnic-like on the polished plum mahogany of the Ketterings' beautiful table. Josie seemed oblivious, but Howard clearly wasn't happy. He gave Carla an apologetic nod, then returned to his attempt to talk Josie into diverting some of the fish for human use.

"We haven't had trout all summer," he complained. "There's enough food in that box for the roses and our dinner, too."

"I won't have time to cook tonight," Josie told him, spearing a pickle with her fork. "I have a Historical Society meeting this afternoon, and then I have to stop by Marge Loden's house.

She promised me some cuttings. Not that I'm going to use them, but she meant well and I couldn't turn her down. You know how Marge loves to talk; she'll keep me there for hours. Why don't you pick up some fried chicken on your way home from the office?"

"All right." Howard was resigned. "I guess I'll just order trout the next time we go to a restaurant.

"Oh, honey! I didn't realize it meant so much to you. I'll put a couple of Carla's fish in the refrigerator and we'll have them tomorrow. We'll have trout for breakfast! As if we were camping. Remember those camping trips you used to take me on when we were younger? All those mosquitos." She patted his hand and sighed. "I never seem to have time to cook these days. There's always so much to do in the summer."

"So much that you want to do, you mean." Howard gave Carla a conspiratorial smile. "Josie isn't happy unless she's crammed one thing too many into her busy schedule."

"She has a lot of energy," Carla said politely, reflecting that it would be a good thing if some of Josie's energy were redirected. She spent far too much of it in lording it over the residents of Placer Bar.

"I'm a lucky man." Howard's smile grew tender as it widened to include his wife. "There are more important things in life than trout for dinner."

Then his expression turned serious. "I suppose the police have talked to you about the murder."

"I think they've interviewed everybody who attended the Stauffers's party."

"I ran into Lieutenant Pressner this morning. He wouldn't tell me very much about the investigation, but I got the impression that he's treating Owen as a serious suspect." Howard's tone was indignant. Carla couldn't figure out if he was upset because the cop had refused to share sensitive police information, treating him like an ordinary citizen, or if he objected to Pressner's attitude toward Owen.

"At least they haven't arrested Owen, or they hadn't last night," she offered. "I helped him move into the Miner's Palace Hotel."

"Really?" Howard wiped a trace of mustard from his mouth and leaned forward. "Did he mention anything about his plans?"

"He's still bringing the factory here, if that's what you mean. He said his company is committed to the move now that they've purchased the land."

"Thank goodness!" he exclaimed. "Everyone in town is counting on the new jobs. I know a couple of people personally who've traded their cars in on new ones, figuring they'll make enough extra money to swing the payments. Foolish, of course, but you can't stop them from doing it. We'd have been in big trouble if Owen had pulled out at this point." Even Josie seemed pleased.

"You know, the Police Chief is an old friend of mine," he went on. "I think I'll have a word with him, suggest that he tell Pressner to be a little more tactful about the way he handles this case. Owen Stauffer has been through a terrible experience and we don't want to upset him any more than necessary."

"You're going to ask the cops to call off their investigation?" Carla's voice rose in astonishment.

"No, no, nothing like that. But in this country a man is presumed innocent until proven guilty. I'm all for law and order, but that doesn't mean the police should be allowed to go around harassing people."

Not if their victims were rich and influential, at least. Carla wondered if Howard would feel so strongly about individual

196

rights if Steve Rucker were the cops's main suspect. She fought down the temptation to ask. She was a guest in the Ketterings's house, after all.

"It sounds as if they've been treating Owen abominably. Simply persecuting the poor man! We ought to do something to let him know we're standing behind him." Josie's eyes glowed with righteous fervor. "I know! Let's throw a dinner party in his honor."

Josie's desire to run things knew no limit, Carla reflected with amusement. Now she'd decided to appoint herself Owen's champion.

Howard nodded absently and turned to Carla. "Do you have any idea what Owen intends to do with Granddad's old house?"

"The Kettering mansion? He's putting it on the market."

Josie snorted. "I'm glad to hear it. I've always said the restoration project was a silly idea. The house is just too far gone to be saved. Still, I suppose the lot has some value. You could build a small subdivision if you tore the house down. And there'll be plenty of demand for housing with the new factory."

Carla had been exorcised of her compulsive urge to possess the house, but she still loved and admired the proud old building. She found Josie's enthusiasm for leveling the place strongly offensive. She'd finished her sandwich and now she rose to her feet. "I must be going," she told Josie. "It sounds like you have a busy afternoon ahead of you."

Howard showed her to the door. "Maybe you and your husband could come when we hold the dinner party for Owen," he suggested. "It's important to present a united front."

"I'll mention it to Peter," she promised.

It was starting to sound as if Owen wasn't going to need much defending, Carla reflected as she set off down the sidewalk. From what she'd seen, the townspeople had grouped themselves firmly behind him. Ned had scoffed at the idea that Owen might be the killer, calling it a crazy idea. All he cared about at this point was landing a job as one of the contractors building the factory. Sally was in love with the man, so of course she wouldn't listen to a word against him, and Maud didn't particularly care if he'd murdered Bronwin or not. The Ketterings had taken Owen's side because they didn't want the town to lose the jobs he carried in his pocket. Even Pat Graedon, the leader of the faction opposing the factory, had nothing but sympathy for Owen's personal plight. The impossible Lieutenant Pressner seemed to be the only person left in town who was willing to believe that Owen might be a killer, and if so, should be punished for his crime.

Carla didn't like it. For one thing, while she found Owen very likable personally, she wanted to see him brought to justice if he was guilty. For another, most of his supporters seemed to be motivated by self-interest, and that sort of thing can turn around in a hurry. Well, not with Sally. It was unlikely that she'd change her mind. But the rest of the town probably wouldn't be so consistent. Once the factory was up and running and the promised new jobs were secured, new rumors would start. Rumors to the effect that the investigation had been quashed because of Owen's influence in Placer Bar. Even if Owen was innocent, he would suffer. He'd be under suspicion for the rest of his life.

But what could she do to stop this? Nothing. She'd talked to everyone she knew who'd been at the party and she was no closer to finding the real killer than she'd been on the night that Bronwin was murdered.

As she passed the hardware store, she noticed a poster in the window. It advertised the Grand Opening of the Ebbets Mine, to be held the very next day. Get with the program, she told herself. Owen's problems were really none of her business and she'd been neglecting her own responsibilities. Peter would expect her to go to the mine opening with him, partly for fun and partly so he could put in an appearance as one of the town's movers and shakers. She should have made plans to meet him, perhaps to pack a picnic lunch. It wouldn't hurt her to pay a little attention to their marriage for a change.

Chapter 20

The phone was ringing as Carla let herself into her house. She hurried through the living room to answer it.

"Ms. Weber?" The voice at the other end of the line was diffident. "I'm sorry to disturb you, but I wondered if I could have my ledger back. Surely you've had time to look through it. It makes me nervous, having the book out of the shop this way. I like to keep my financial records together in one place, where I can get at them if I need to."

Her mind didn't make the connection for a minute, but then she realized she was talking to Mr. Large, the owner of the semi-derelict hardware store. "Yes, of course. Your ledger and the wallpaper catalogs. I'm sorry I've kept them so long. I don't have the books in my hands right now, but I'll get them back to you as soon as possible." Evidently Mr. Large hadn't heard about the murder, or if he had, he didn't realize that his books were connected with the case in any way. Carla was not about to upset him by giving him the bad news.

"I suppose there's no hurry, not with the catalogs." An apologetic note entered his voice. "It's the ledger I'm worried about. The IRS, you know. I wanted to make sure the ledger was all right in case they showed up and asked to see it."

"I can return all the books, the ledger and the catalogs as well," she repeated. "I've finished my research project." The new buyers of the Kettering mansion were hardly likely to want to do a historically correct restoration job, and if they did want to, she could always borrow the books again. They'd be safe enough in their original cupboard.

She cut short Mr. Large's protestations of gratitude and put in a call to the Miner's Palace Hotel. She'd need Owen's keys to get into the Mother Lode Lake house to pick up Mr. Large's books.

Pat Graedon answered the phone. "Owen isn't here right now. I told him he was making a mistake, but he insisted on driving in to work this afternoon. Said he had some urgent things to take care of at his Sacramento office."

Her voice rose in indignation. "That poor man! You wouldn't believe the way the police are behaving. They have him under surveillance! A cop's been sitting in the lobby all morning. When I asked him what he was doing, he said he was waiting for a friend. He was dressed in plain clothes, but he was with the police, I could tell. When Owen went out to his car, the man tailed him. And he must have radioed in a report that Owen was leaving, because the next thing you know, Lieutenant Pressner showed up and asked if he could look through Owen's room while he was gone. I told him to get a search warrant. My guests are entitled to their privacy, just like everyone else!"

Carla expressed her sympathy and hung up the phone. There went her opportunity of delivering the ledger that afternoon. She felt disappointed by the setback. She'd been looking forward to accomplishing something constructive. Still, there was no help for it. She'd have to wait until evening when she could get the keys from Owen.

Or—would she? She retrieved a dim visual memory from the night of Bronwin's death. She'd been standing back near the stairs, watching as Steve Rucker performed artificial respiration,

pressing the shoulders of the drowned woman's still form. The
white wire table next to the chaise longue had been in her line
of sight and there'd been a dark rectangular blur on the table's
mesh surface—the ledger and the catalogs, and Bronwin's fashion magazines, of course. Bronwin had left Mr. Large's books
outside, probably since the day Carla had given them to her, and
unless the police had taken them away as evidence, they'd still
be there, out in the back yard. She wouldn't need a key, after
all.

She dialed Peter's number and arranged to borrow his car,
then hurried down to his office to pick up the Nissan.

She'd forgotten about the guard at the subdivision gate.
He insisted on checking with Owen at his office in Sacramento.
This took a while, but the guard finally obtained permission to
let her through. She drove up the hill.

The house looked innocuous enough from the street, just
another overgrown suburban residence, but her heart thumped
unpleasantly as she went around through the side yard. Her
knees were weak with the memory of fear by the time she
reached the pool. She sank down onto Bronwin's plastic chaise
to recover.

She snatched the ledger from the wire table, hoping to distract herself from her morbid thoughts. The book fell open at
the Kettering order. She glanced through the entries. The ledger
listed enough building materials construct a dozen houses like
the one she shared with Peter, but the total bill came to less than
eight thousand dollars. Of course, that had been a whole lot of
money back in 1864.

She closed the book and her mind returned to the murder.
She conjured up the living room as it had looked when she and
Peter arrived at the Stauffers's party. Owen had been standing
near the table that held the factory model, flushed with success.

Maud Rucker chatted with her elderly male friend while Steve lurked against a far wall. Josie and Howard had been in a huddle with Pat Graedon near the front door. Then she thought of Bronwin as she'd looked when she was pulled from the pool, her slim, silver-clad body lying drowned on the blue and orange tiles.

Carla jumped to her feet, clutching the ledger hard against her breast. She knew what had happened—who had killed Bronwin and why the man in the military jacket had been murdered. She even knew why the fire had been set.

The trouble was, she had no proof. But—yes, there might be a way to strengthen her case. She would have to get her hands on the first dead body, the mummified corpse she'd found in the linen closet.

How could she do this? She supposed the cops were holding the dead man somewhere, in custody, so to speak, in the hope that someone would come forward to identify him. Surely they hadn't shipped him to Sacramento. But how could she gain access to the corpse?

She decided that her best bet would be to approach the young cop, the blond ex-football star. He'd seemed sympathetic and not overly sharp. Grabbing the ledger and the wallpaper catalogs, she ran around the side of the house to her car.

Carla was in luck. The young cop was on desk duty again and there was no one else in the police station lobby. His face lit up in welcome as she pushed through the heavy glass door. She was definitely one of his favorite customers.

She approached the desk slowly, assuming a diffident air. "I'm sorry to bother you, but I'm afraid I've come up with another problem. I suppose this may sound a little strange—"

The cop's eyes widened in greedy anticipation. What *new* horror was she about to produce?

"It's the dead man I found in the linen closet. I can't seem to get him out of my mind. I dream about him every night. Somehow he's become—well, an important player in my life, you might say. I thought if I could only take a look at him, it might help me to regain some sense of perspective."

"I see what you mean." The cop pursed his lips thoughtfully. This was an awfully weak story, but he was treating her with perfect seriousness.

"We're holding him down at Samson's Mortuary," he told her. "I suppose he doesn't really need the refrigeration facilities, but we turn all our dead bodies over to them for storage. I tell you what. I get off duty in another hour. I could take you over there if you like."

"Could you? I'd be very grateful." She glanced at her watch. "I have a few things to take care of in the meantime. Why don't I meet you at the funeral parlor. At four o'clock?" Carla didn't really have any errands to run, but she was afraid that Lieutenant Pressner might walk into the lobby and demand to know why she was hanging around the police station. She had a good idea that he wouldn't approve of her arrangement with the young cop.

She used the free time to make a quick detour home, where she pocketed a set of sharp nail clippers from her manicure kit.

* * *

The funeral parlor occupied a big turreted frame house in the old part of town. The young cop was waiting at the door. The overdressed and somewhat harassed-looking receptionist didn't seem at all surprised by his request to see the body. She led them to the basement without questioning their reason for being there.

The receptionist used a key to let them into a tile-floored room. Skirting a steel examining table, she walked over to the far wall and pulled out a large metal drawer, one of a low bank of five. "Push the drawer in when you're through," she told them, and returned to her post.

Carla's memory was disappointingly accurate. The man's jacket was definitely a light brown color. It was made of rough wool, worn and a little mottled in places, but she really couldn't bring herself to believe that it had faded to this shade from pale gray. Damn! She doubled up her fists in frustration.

Misinterpreting her emotion, the young man moved closer and laid a comforting hand on her shoulder. "He never loses his fascination, does he?" he confided. "I come here often just to look at him."

So that was why the receptionist hadn't questioned their visit. She must have assumed he'd come here to share his favorite corpse with a friend. Carla wondered if he'd been bringing his dates to the funeral parlor.

"That's an unusual jacket he's wearing," she remarked, trying to shift the conversation back into normal channels. "I mean, the jacket itself is made of cheap material, but the gold braid is extremely opulent." The inch-wide strip of braid looped down the dead man's sleeve in a series of extravagant whirls and flourishes extending from above his elbows down to his cuffs. "The braid must have cost more than the jacket itself. And look—the braid is tacked on with big sloppy stitches, as if it had been taken from another garment."

"Yeah, and the yellow satin collar and cuffs are tacked on, too, now that you mention it."

Carla sighed and took a step backward. "Well, I guess I've seen enough. This should help me sleep a little better tonight."

Then she glanced at the floor beyond the young cop's back and twisted her mouth into a horrified expression. "Oh, no! Rats!"

"Where?" He jerked around to look, his hand moving

instinctively to his gun.

"Over there. They ran behind that cabinet!"

The cop hunched his shoulders into a crouch. As he crept across the floor to investigate, Carla reached out with the nail clippers she held palmed in her hand and snipped loose a section of brown cloth from a ripped spot on the front of the jacket. She stuffed this into her jeans pocket, then clipped off a section of gold braid and a piece of the yellow collar fabric for good measure.

By the time the cop decided it was a false alarm, Carla was pushing the heavy steel drawer back into the wall unit. "I guess I must have been seeing things," she told him with an apologetic smile. "We'd better go before my imagination gets the best of me again."

Carla carried her prizes home and examined them unhappily. A few scraps of wallpaper, some shreds of brown cloth—it wasn't much to go on. What she needed now was expert advice. She put in a call to Pat at the Miner's Palace Hotel.

"I've been trying to decide what to do. A friend of mine found an interesting looking military uniform at the bottom of an old trunk she picked up at an auction. It's probably just a costume party piece, but if it's an authentic antique, you might be able to talk her into donating it to the Clampers for this museum you say they're starting. Is there anybody involved with the organization I could talk to about this?"

"Hold on a minute." Pat covered the receiver with her hand. Carla heard a muffled conversation on the other end of the line, and then she spoke again. "Lucas said that you might want to consult Jacob Lindstrom. He's our local expert on military history."

Pat gave her an address out on Ridge Road. Carla jumped back into Peter's car. Mr. Lindstrom was at home, watching daytime television in the snug pine-paneled living room of his small house. He was an elderly man with a long, thin face, distinguished-looking in tweed trousers and a beige cardigan. Leather slip-ons covered his narrow feet.

Carla repeated her story about finding the uniform in a trunk. It sounded like a fib, even to her, but she thought it might make a poor impression if she admitted she'd been robbing the dead, that she'd snipped her ghastly souvenirs from a corpse. Perhaps she could talk the cops into donating the uniform to the Clampers when the case was closed, she told herself, trying to rationalize telling lies to a stranger.

Mr. Lindstrom's eyes gleamed with interest as she described the jacket—the cheap brown material, the loops of rich gold braid tacked to the sleeves, the three bars on the yellow satin collar. When she handed him a plastic bag containing the snippets of fabric, he fingered the sorry scraps with reverence.

"It sounds like your friend has a Civil War uniform on her hands. A captain's uniform, to judge from the three bars."

"But the jacket was brown."

He nodded sagely. "Confederate."

"But the Confederates wore gray," she argued with rising excitement. "As opposed to the Union blue. That's how the Blue and the Gray Cemetery on the outskirts of town got its name."

"That's what the soldiers were supposed to wear, but you have to understand—towards the end of the war, the Confederacy ran low on supplies, and one of the things they were short of was gray cloth. They started dying their uniforms with nut shells and iron filings. 'Butternut', that's what they called the resulting light brown color. From what you tell me, I'd say we're talking about a replacement jacket. The original wore out, or it was hopelessly soaked with blood, or it simply became too filthy to clean or to wear, and the owner transferred the cuffs and gold braid to a new, makeshift uniform. I'd be willing to bet that your friend has found a genuine relic of the Civil War. I don't need to tell you that the Clampers would be delighted to accept such a gift."

This was exactly what Carla had been hoping to hear. "I'll be in touch," she promised. She was finally ready to go to the police.

Chapter 21

It was after five o'clock, but Lieutenant Pressner was still in his office. Carla had to run through her story several times before he fully understood what she was saying, and even then he was incredulous.

"Your theory just doesn't sound right to me," he complained. "And I don't like your plan, either. What are you trying to do here, cause trouble for everybody?"

"Only for the murderer. Just be there at the Ebbets Mine opening tomorrow to back me up. That's all I ask. You'll see that I'm right. The killer is bound to show up for the ceremony, and we'll have a whole mine full of witnesses if I can extract a confession."

"I suppose I can't stop you." He sighed impatiently. "I have to be there anyway. I'll see you tomorrow."

This was as much of a commitment as she was going to get from him, Carla realized. She thanked him for his time. Pressner refused to accept custody of Mr. Large's old ledger and the scraps of cloth from the Civil War, so she took them home with her after she left the police station.

The ledger and the few snippets of material were the only concrete evidence she had, she reflected as she walked back to the Nissan. She really ought to put them in a safe place. The vault down at Peter's savings and loan office would be ideal, of course, but she'd have to enlist his help to open the door, so that was out. She had no intention of letting her husband in on her plan. He'd only try to talk her out of it.

No, she resolved, she would keep her theory a secret until Pressner had arrested the murderer. Then it would be too late for Peter to interfere.

She locked the books and the fabric scraps in Peter's car trunk. It seemed like her best alternative under the circumstances.

* * *

Carla had trouble getting to sleep that night. She lay in bed, stiff with tension, well into the small hours. She finally drifted off, but she jerked awake with the coming of dawn. She crept out of bed and prepared an elaborate breakfast, using the empty time to mix up a batch of homemade muffins and squeeze some oranges. Peter had a smile on his face when she saw him off to work. The rest of the morning passed with excruciating slowness until finally ten o'clock rolled around, the time of the mine opening ceremony.

Peter considered attending these occasions to be part of his job, and he liked her to show up, too. She met him by arrangement at the tiny park marking the head of the mine shaft. The mine opening had attracted a lot of attention. Half the town had turned out and the streets were jammed with onlookers.

Carla peered around anxiously to see if she could spot the murderer, rising on tiptoe and craning to see over people's heads. The Graedons were sitting on a makeshift platform with the Mayor and some of the other town officials and prominent citizens. Ned and Sally were talking to the Ketterings over near the entrance to the mine. As she pulled Peter in the direction of this second group, she caught sight of Maud and Steve Rucker coming down Broad Street. Owen was the only person missing. He'd probably gone to work at his office in Sacramento, she decided.

The speeches lasted for nearly an hour. Carla was too nervous to follow the sense of them. The Mayor, a grizzled old fellow who looked as if he might have worked in the mine once himself, finally stepped forward to cut the red ribbon.

As the thin strand parted, a tremendous thumping noise began. The sound was deafening. Blow after heavy blow rang out, literally shaking the ground. The assembled people swayed as if buffeted by a rolling tide, raising their hands to cover their ears.

Thoroughly unnerved by the unexpected uproar, Carla looked around for the source of the noise. Her eyes finally settled on the old stamp mill at the edge of the park. She'd noticed the stamp mill before, but she hadn't realized that it was still operational. Somebody had hooked it up to a generator and pushed the on switch in a misguided attempt to add a little color to the mine opening ceremony.

As she watched, the four pistons with heavy foot-high cylindrical steel weights at their ends smashed rhythmically down, hitting the metal base plate with a resounding crash, then drew up into their frame again to prepare for another descent. The machine's purpose was to crush big chunks of gold ore, grinding them into a powder to prepare them for leaching. Nobody was feeding rocks into the hopper, so there was nothing to soften the bellowing clang of steel against steel.

Recovering from the first shock of the tremendous noise, the crowd surged toward the mine entrance as if seeking shelter from the blows of sound. Peter grabbed Carla's wrist to keep her from being torn away, and Ned put his hands on Sally's shoulders. The four of them managed to stay together as they were pushed forward by the people behind them. The mine carts somewhat resembled the cars on a roller coaster, open gondolas with rows of bench seats, mounted on metal rails. Carla and

211

Peter clambered into the first cart for the ride down the shaft, sitting behind Maud and Steve Rucker and the Ketterings. Sally and Ned got in beside them. Carla looked around for the Graedons, but they were nowhere in sight. They were probably still marooned on the platform with the Mayor, she realized. The rest of the cart filled up quickly, mainly with young teenagers in Boy Scout uniforms.

Electric lights had been installed in the tunnel, illuminating the new wood that lined the walls and ceiling to prevent cave-ins. The roar of the stamp machine didn't fade as the cart started down the track. Instead, the noise rolled off the walls, even more overwhelming as it echoed through the low-ceilinged claustrophobic space.

The cart didn't run very quickly, but the descent was steep. Carla's heart was in her throat by the time they reached the bottom of the mine shaft. She climbed out on rubbery legs. They had reached a large chamber far beneath the ground.

Lieutenant Pressner was there already, arms folded, waiting in front of a row of display cases holding picks and lamps and other bits of old mining gear. Carla caught his eye and smiled in greeting. He shifted his weight, looking uncomfortable, but at least he was here for her as he had promised.

Peter and the others pushed forward to examine the relics on display. Carla plucked Josie's sleeve. When she'd planned this encounter she'd imagined herself as a cool and subtle inquisitor, a superior Bronwin-esque figure, but she had to scream to make herself heard over the crash of the stamp machine. "I need to talk to you for a moment."

Josie raised her eyebrows, then gave a short nod.

Conversation was impossible in the main room of the mine. Carla wasn't happy about it, but she pulled the older woman to a side tunnel branching off to the right, hoping to get away from the worst of the noise. The passageway curved sharply after about ten feet. The thudding roar still followed them, but once they'd rounded the bend it was possible to talk without stripping their throats raw with the effort.

"What's on your mind? I really need to get back to Howard." The lights were much dimmer here than in the main room, just a single bulb mounted on the roof of the mine. It was hard for Carla to make out Josie's expression.

Carla glanced back in the direction from which they'd come. A shadow moved on the wall just beyond the bend, long legs scissoring. A man had followed them into the side tunnel. It had to be Lieutenant Pressner. Reassured, she turned to face Josie.

"I know you killed Bronwin." Carla's voice cracked with compassion. She was ruining Josie's life, about to destroy the other woman completely. The responsibility weighed on her. She remembered how she'd felt when she'd thought that *she* was guilty of murder. She would have done anything to escape punishment, to avoid paying the price for one tragic mistake.

"I'm so terribly sorry that I have to turn you in," she went on. "Bronwin put you in an awful position, I know. I can't let you get away with killing her, though. For one thing, that would leave Owen as the main suspect. He'd never be able to clear himself."

"What are you talking about?" Josie moved a step closer. She raised her hands as if to ward off a blow.

Carla was suddenly conscious that Josie outweighed her by at least fifty pounds. The older woman was a menacing figure. Intimidated, she stepped back a couple of paces. Something cold and hard hit her across the small of the back, forcing her to a stop.

She looked over her shoulder and broke into a sweat of terror. She was standing at the edge of a pit, the narrow entrance to a vertical shaft plunging down to a lower section of the mine, guarded by nothing more than an iron railing. The fall looked impressive; she couldn't see the bottom of the hole.

Carla was appalled. How had she put herself in this dangerous situation? She should have talked somebody into letting her visit the mine before the ceremony, so she could check out the terrain. Her plan had been to force Josie into a confession, and she'd been worried that the other woman would deny everything. Now her goal was simple survival. She was terrified that Josie would prove her guilt by committing another murder before Lieutenant Pressner could rush forward to save her.

She inched sideways, her back pressed against the railing, trying to dodge to Josie's left. "I've found documentary evidence," she panted, hoping to distract her adversary. "An old ledger that shows the date the mansion was built. And I know who killed the man in the military jacket. I talked to an expert who identified the dead man as a Confederate Captain, a soldier from the Civil War." She'd managed to move away a few paces from the terrifying hole, but how far, she didn't know.

Josie gave a strangled yell, then brought her voice back under control. "Outsiders," she hissed. "How I hate you people from the big city. You move to Placer Bar and ruin everything. You don't understand our ways and you don't respect them."

Her hands flew out unexpectedly and she grabbed Carla's wrists. Josie lunged forward, throwing all her weight into the move.

Carla was taken by surprise, and she staggered backward. To her horror, Josie had shoved her up against the guardrail again. Josie was surprisingly strong and her extra weight gave her a decisive advantage. Carla pushed back as hard as she could, but her straining opponent didn't budge an inch.

She kicked out in desperation, hoping to catch the older woman on the shin, but the attempt knocked her off balance. This was the chance that Josie had been waiting for. Her next

214

shove sent Carla sprawling back over the rail. She would have fallen if she hadn't managed to hook her right foot behind one of the upright metal support posts.

She screamed, putting all her strength into the cry for help. She knew she couldn't be heard in the main chamber over the tremendous rolling noise of the stamp mill, and she prayed that she hadn't been imagining things when she'd seen the shadow of a man against the wall.

Time slowed, stretching into an agonizing eternity as she looked into Josie's sweat-beaded face. Josie's features were set in lines of hard determination. Her breath fanned Carla's cheek as they both gasped for air. Carla managed to keep her foot wrapped around the support post by an effort of will, but she knew it was only a matter of seconds before Josie would send her plunging into the void.

A cloud passed in front of her eyes and the deep boom of the stamp mill faded away into a hollow clatter. Then the noise resolved into the sound of running footsteps, pounding down the tunnel floor.

Josie disappeared from view and Carla fell forward. She found herself on her hands and knees, staring at one of Peter's shoes—a black loafer. She recognized it by the scuff mark he'd picked up changing a flat tire the week before.

She raised her head and looked at him. Peter was bending toward her, holding out his hand. He'd pushed Josie aside and she was crouched panting on the floor near the left wall of the side tunnel.

"Are you all right?" Peter seemed more astonished than frightened. He hadn't taken it all in yet. "What's going on here? Has everyone gone crazy?"

Half a dozen Boy Scouts ran into the chamber, whooping loudly, egging each other on, each one competing to act the sillier. They were followed by Lieutenant Pressner. Peter must have attracted their attention when he ran to her aid, Carla reflected woozily.

She took her husband's hand and lurched to her feet. "Arrest Josie Kettering for the murder of Bronwin Stauffer," she told the startled policeman. "And if you aren't willing to do that, arrest her for trying to kill me. My husband was a witness to her last attempt at murder."

"Murder?" Peter's face was a mask of astonishment.

"Where were you when I needed protection?" she shouted at the Lieutenant. Then she burst into tears.

Chapter 22

Peter put a comforting hand on Carla's shoulder. They turned to look at Josie. She'd regained her feet by now and there was a peculiar expression on her face. Under their scrutiny, her mouth began to work convulsively, as if she were rehearsing an explanation or an excuse.

Lieutenant Pressner took a couple of steps in Josie's direction, giving her a reassuring smile. Misinterpreting his intentions, she flinched away with a cry. Her back hit the iron railing, hard. The bolts holding it to the floor of the mine weren't anchored very well, and they must have been weakened by the repeated blows Carla had given them as she struggled with Josie. A long section of railing fell away, sagging into the hole.

Josie swayed, off-balance. She stood upright for a moment, poised over the void, and then she gave a deep sigh and her body relaxed. She deliberately abandoned herself to the fall.

Carla ran forward, her eyes straining into the deep blackness. Peter and the Lieutenant were close behind her. There was a series of sickening muffled thumps as Josie's falling body ricocheted off the walls of the vertical tunnel. The hair on Carla's arms prickled in the chill air that rose from the dark pit. It seemed like a long time before they heard Josie hit the bottom.

Carla slumped against Peter. "She's dead." She was too drained to feel much more than a sense of relief at her delivery from danger.

Pressner's eyes were wide with shock, but he quickly recovered. He knew how to deal with this kind of an emergency. "We'll need a rescue team to get her out of there," he barked. "I'll have to call in the Fire Department."

They had all forgotten about the Boy Scouts. The youngsters stood huddled against the far wall, completely silent. They looked like a flock of owls, hypnotized into immobility by a bright searchlight. Compressing his lips in disapproval, Pressner herded them ahead of him into the main chamber as he went to summon help.

Carla knew that she and Peter should leave, too, but she couldn't bring herself to go back into the main room. She couldn't shake the nightmare fear that Josie would crawl up out of the mine shaft and come after her again. The experience wasn't over for her; she needed to see the body.

Peter seemed to understand. He waited with her patiently, his hands on her shoulders.

She was very glad to have him there for support when Howard shuffled into the chamber. His face was stark white and he seemed to move with an effort, using his last reserves of strength. Ignoring them, he went to the section of railing that still stood upright and hunched over it as if in terrible physical pain.

Pressner must have established communication with the outside world, for the thumping of the stamp machine cut off with a final tremendous bang. It left an aching void behind it, as if the life support system that had kept them going had suddenly been taken away.

Carla's chest flooded with emotion as the pity she'd ceased to feel for Josie threatened to overwhelm her. Howard Kettering had loved his wife. He'd known that she'd killed Bronwin and he'd tried to protect her. He'd tried to protect Owen, too. She'd misjudged Howard when she'd thought he was motivated by business reasons when he'd asked the police to drop Owen as a suspect. He hadn't wanted to see an innocent man accused of Josie's crime.

Pressner marched back into the side tunnel, followed by a crew of firemen. Retrieving the body was not an easy job. The pit was too deep for the firemen's ladders, so they had to lower a man on a rope. It took almost an hour to secure Josie's body and winch it up.

Howard's face was impassive as he gazed at the blanket-wrapped figure lying on the floor of the mine, but his voice was harsh and he spoke with an effort. "I'd appreciate it if you could release the body as soon as possible. I'll want to give my wife a proper burial."

"There's an ambulance at the head of the mine shaft. You don't look well. Maybe you should let them take you to the hospital, along with Josie." Pressner reached forward to take Howard by the arm, but the other man jerked away.

"I'll be all right. I know I'll have to talk to you sooner or later, and I'd just as soon get it over with."

"You're sure you're up to it?"

Howard Kettering didn't respond. Pressner gave a small shrug. "Meet me at the top of the shaft, then. I'll be up in a few minutes."

Howard plodded back into the main chamber. Carla and Peter followed him. The mine had been cleared of celebrants and the mine cart was waiting at the bottom of the rails. Howard gave no sign that he was aware of their presence as he climbed into the front of the cart. Respecting his grief, they took a seat at the rear. Peter pressed a switch on the wall to signal the engine operator at the top of the shaft that they were ready to go. The cart whined into motion.

Pressner rode up in the cart a few minutes later. The four of them drove to the police station in silence. Pressner beckoned to a uniformed man to join them as he led the way to his office.

The uniformed man produced a couple of extra plastic-seated metal chairs and they sat in a semi-circle in front of Pressner's desk. Pressner went over to a file cabinet and took out a bottle of brandy. He grabbed a handful of paper cups from a water cooler in the corner and filled a cup with the amber liquid. He handed it to Howard Kettering, who took a long shuddering gulp.

Pressner sat down at his desk and flicked on a tape recorder. Then his eyes fell on the china Buddha; he tucked the figurine into a desk drawer. Carla was very glad he'd done this. It would have been unbearable to give a statement with the figurine looking on, smiling idiotically and nodding its jointed head.

She cleared her throat and shifted in her chair, thoroughly miserable by now. There seemed no words for what she had to say. "I'm sorry. I didn't mean for her to die." She couldn't meet Howard's eyes.

"You didn't push her." His voice was desolate, but he didn't seem bitter. "If only Josie hadn't set that fire. Then when she killed Bronwin—" He spread his hands helplessly. "I don't think she really wanted to live after that."

"Wait a minute," Pressner broke in. "You're confirming Ms. Weber's allegation that Mrs. Kettering was the murderer?" He still didn't really believe it. His eyes darted nervously to Carla's face, then returned to Howard. "And what's all this about a fire? Are you talking about the fire at the Kettering mansion?"

"The vandalism at the mansion and Bronwin's death were linked together." Carla decided to help Howard out with his explanation. "The whole thing was a cover-up," she went on, her voice growing in strength. "A cover-up leading to a bigger cover-up, until it got out of hand and ended in the final cover-up, murder."

The Lieutenant still looked incredulous, but she had his full attention. "Josie Kettering was a proud woman, and the main source of her pride was the Kettering family's position in this community. Her own parents had been poor and, I gather, somewhat disreputable, which only made her take more pleasure in the Kettering name. Maintaining her husband's prestige was the most important thing in her life.

"Part of the Kettering legend was the story of Davis Kettering, a Southern gentleman who came to California and founded the family's fortunes after fighting in the Civil War. Josie always spoke of him as the romantic cavalier type, a dashing soldier who only turned to business after his cause was irretrievably lost—and who went on to distinguish himself in peace time, accumulating honors and a huge fortune."

Her voice grew thin with sympathy, but she forced herself to continue. "The story was a lie. The Kettering mansion was built in 1864, a year before the Civil War ended. If Davis Kettering fought for the South, he had to be a deserter. And that raises the interesting question: How could he have come to California with enough money in his pocket to construct a house like the Kettering mansion?"

"That's the way it happened." Howard took up the tale. He sounded musing, as if the events he related had no connection to him or his late wife. "My grandfather made a full confession to me the night he died. He didn't get along with my father very well, and I guess he sensed he didn't have much longer to live. I was just a kid at the time, but I was the one sitting by the side of his hospital bed and he selected me to hear his story. He wanted to clear his conscience.

"It seems that my grandfather emigrated to this country from England just as the Civil War was breaking out. He joined the Confederate forces because he thought the South would win, and serving as a soldier would help him get established in his new land. He was a sort of mercenary on the Confederate side, you might say."

Pressner leaned forward to refill Howard's paper cup with brandy. Howard took a sip before he continued.

"As the war dragged on, Davis became disillusioned with the Southern cause. The conflict had lasted a lot longer than he expected. His company wasn't receiving proper food or clothing, much less the pay they'd been promised, and he began to realize that the South was bound to lose. Even if he managed to stay alive, his military service wouldn't be of help to him when the war ended. He decided to desert.

"The trouble was, he didn't have any money—certainly not enough to pay his passage home. Then he stumbled across a chance to become a purchasing agent for the Confederate Army. He persuaded his Captain to entrust him with a large sum of gold to buy arms in England. He told the man he had business connections in Liverpool and could get the guns at a good price. But instead of taking ship for England, he slipped onto a boat headed for California. He figured by the time his fellow soldiers realized they'd been cheated, it would be too late for them to do anything about it."

Howard stopped talking, as though the story were over. "That's where the body in the linen closet comes in," Carla explained. "Davis's Captain must have had his suspicions. He followed him to California and tried to get the money back. Davis managed to get in the first shot, though."

Carla realized that her voice had grown a little too eager. She went on, subdued. "I knew that Davis had killed the man in

222

the military jacket because the corpse was walled up in the house itself. If Davis had buried him outside, even on the grounds, anybody might have dug him up—a gardener, a servant digging a grave for a dead pet, a visiting child excavating a flower bed just for the fun of it. But nobody was going to go tearing down Davis's walls without his permission. I expect he stashed the Captain's corpse somewhere after he first murdered him, then put him in the linen closet after the house was built. He decided it was the safest way to hide the body permanently."

Howard's fist closed convulsively and he dropped the crumpled paper cup on the floor. "Grandfather told me he'd killed the man. I didn't know he'd hidden the body in the house until after Carla found him."

"It all hangs together," Carla said to herself. "I kept thinking that the fire was connected to the murder of the man in the military jacket, but I couldn't figure out why the killer hadn't simply taken the body away. Everyone in town knew that Bronwin intended to renovate the mansion, and any secrets hidden in the house would be revealed. But the fire took place after the body had been found. Then it came to me—the person who set the fire wasn't the killer, and hadn't even known where the body was buried. They just wanted to stop people like me from asking questions."

Howard took up the thread of the story again. "Davis invested his stolen gold wisely. One of the first things he did was to construct the house, a suitable home for a prosperous businessman. He was in a hurry to establish himself as a respectable gentleman of means, on the theory that this would put him in a strong position if the murder were discovered. When it comes to punishing crimes, people have always been reluctant to accuse the rich and influential."

Lieutenant Pressner flushed. He was probably remembering his refusal to take the banker's wife seriously as a suspect. Carla realized now that he'd agreed to meet her at the mine only because he wanted to stop her from making a scene. He'd known Josie all his life and considered her the pinnacle of respectability. She, Carla, was a stranger in town and he hadn't taken her story seriously.

She looked away tactfully. "It must have been a terrible blow to Josie when she found out that Davis was a criminal."

"I shouldn't have told her!" Howard clenched his fists. "It just popped out one day! You have to understand, Josie and I got married in the 1950's. The Cold War was going strong and Josie was a leader in the civil defense movement. She built a bomb shelter in our back yard and laid in supplies of food and water, and she urged everybody else in town to do the same. 'How could anyone betray their country?" she asked me one evening. That's when I told her about grandfather.

"I didn't mean anything by it. I thought it was kind of a joke, if you can say that about a murder. After all, it had taken place almost a hundred years earlier. If you tell the average person that one of your ancestors was hanged as a horse thief, they'll think it's amusing, right? It's ancient history.

"But Josie had always taken a tremendous pride in our Southern heritage, and she and her friends were highly patriotic. When she learned that Davis had been a murderer, a traitor and a thief, she was simply overwhelmed. She begged me to keep the story quiet, and of course I agreed.

"I mean, it wasn't as if we could have paid the money back," he added defensively. "Who would we have given it to? Davis's Captain was long since dead, and God only knows where he raised the gold in the first place."

"I didn't think of the Cold War angle," Carla murmured to Peter. He reached over and squeezed her hand.

224

"I blame myself," Howard went on. "I should have told the truth after Davis's funeral. People would have been shocked, sure, but they would have forgotten soon enough. I would have lived down the scandal long ago."

Lieutenant Pressner cleared his throat. "I understand your feelings completely, Mr. Kettering. The last thing you'd want to do after burying your grandfather was to spread defamatory rumors. Davis Kettering was beyond the reach of the law in any case, and it was only natural that you'd want to remember the good things about him and forget his crimes. Besides, you were very young."

Pressner was determined to protect the Ketterings no matter what, Carla reflected. He was constitutionally incapable of believing they could do anything wrong.

Howard had lapsed into silence. Carla took up the slack. "That's why Josie was so upset by Bronwin's plan to restore the mansion. She was terrified that we'd find out when the house had been built, and we'd start asking questions about where Davis got the money. Then when I found the body, Josie panicked. She'd been a bit of a tomboy as a young girl and she used her old tricks to try to drive the Stauffers away from Placer Bar—or away from Davis Kettering's house, at any rate. She scribbled that insulting message on the dining room wall and flushed cement down the toilet. Finally, in desperation, she set fire to the house. She didn't realize that Ned had started spending the night there." Carla repressed a shudder, remembering his close escape.

Pressner leaned forward. "Do you have any proof that Mrs. Kettering was behind the vandalism attempts?"

"Just circumstantial evidence. Ned insisted he'd kept the building securely locked at night, and he's not the type to make careless mistakes. There weren't any signs of a break-in, and we

225

couldn't figure out how the vandals could come and go so freely. But when you realize it was Josie, everything becomes obvious. The lock on the front door was an old one and she still had the key."

Howard nodded. "I recognized her style." His voice grew soft. "She never told me in so many words that she'd set the fire, but she was terribly upset when she realized that Ned had been hurt. For days, she would burst into tears over nothing at all."

"Okay, accepting for the moment that Mrs. Kettering was responsible for the trouble at the mansion, why did she kill Bronwin Stauffer?" Lieutenant Pressner asked.

"It was a senseless tragedy." Carla bowed her head. "Josie was obsessed with the need to hide the Kettering family's shameful history, not to mention the way she herself had been breaking the law by vandalizing the mansion. Bronwin, on the other hand, was furious about the damage to her house. She took the vandalism as a personal insult, and she was determined to put a stop to it." Carla flushed, remembering the part she herself had played in the affair. "I gave Bronwin the weapon she needed, documentation that showed the mansion had been built in 1864. She must have followed my line of reasoning and realized that Josie was her vandal. She didn't understand how desperate Josie had become, how determined to keep her secret, or she would have been more careful.

"Bronwin had a mean streak. She must have asked Josie to meet her down by the pool with the idea of taunting her about the Kettering family. She can't have gotten around to producing the ledger—if she had, Josie would have destroyed the book. She probably just threatened to tell the town the whole story unless Josie behaved herself in the future." Carla shook her head sadly. "Josie lashed out with the rock in a moment of fury. When she realized what she'd done, she tipped her unconscious victim into the swimming pool to make sure she wouldn't live to say who'd attacked her."

Peter had been showing signs of agitation, and now he put in a question. "Carla, whatever possessed you to set up the confrontation down in the mine? Josie had already committed one murder. Surely you must have realized she'd be capable of killing again?"

"It was the only way I could think of to bring Josie's crimes home to her. As I've said, my evidence was circumstantial. A ledger and a mummified corpse in an antique uniform weren't proof of anything. My only chance was to surprise Josie into making a confession, and I figured the mine opening ceremony would be a good place to do it. I thought I'd be safe in a large crowd. Besides, I'd arranged for Lieutenant Pressner to follow us and listen in on the conversation—and rush to my rescue if Josie tried anything dangerous."

She gave him a bitter look. "Where were you anyway?"

"I was keeping an eye on the Boy Scouts," he muttered. "They were talking and laughing among themselves, and I thought they might be planning to steal a souvenir from one of the display cases."

His voice grew stronger. "You have to admit, it was asking a lot to expect me to believe that Josie Kettering had committed a murder. Josie Kettering! I thought you were crazy when you came into my office and started ranting about old ledgers and the Civil War."

Carla glared at him. Then her face softened as she turned to Peter. "Thanks for saving my life."

Chapter 23

Carla and Peter walked home slowly through the bright September afternoon. The weather had changed during the night and fall was coming at last. There was a crisp smell in the air, and soon the trees would start to change. Placer Bar was pretty at this time of the year, she had to admit.

Carla felt sad yet obscurely comforted, as if she'd attended a funeral. Perhaps, as with a funeral, it was the relief of having come through an ordeal. She didn't feel comfortable with Peter, though. The experience they'd just been through had left her strangely shy.

Peter was the first to break the silence. "I have a confession to make. I didn't follow you into that side shaft because I thought you were in danger. The thought never crossed my mind. You'd been giving Josie odd looks all through the Mayor's speech, as if you were angry at her for some reason, and when you drew her aside, I was afraid you might be planning to say something rude. I wanted to be there to smooth things over if you picked a quarrel."

"A quarrel!" she repeated, trying to take in the idea. Then she started to laugh. "Well, you were right. I wasn't very tactful with Josie and I'm sure glad you were there to save the day.

"Say," she went on, sobered by a sudden thought. "You don't think Howard will get into trouble, do you? They won't try to arrest him as an accessory, will they?"

"I'm sure they won't. Husbands can't be forced to testify against their wives, and they certainly can't be required to turn them in to the police.

"I expect he'll have popular sympathy on his side, too," he added. "Most people will feel the way we do. They'll admire Howard for his loyalty."

They walked on a bit further. The sense of constraint was still there between them. "I was impressed by the way you put everything together," Peter offered, obviously reaching for something to say.

"It all fell into place once I realized that the Civil War didn't end until 1865." Privately, Carla could have kicked herself. She should have been quicker to realize what was happening. Lucas Graedon had even shown her a sketch of the Great Scare memorial, with the dates of the war right there on the bronze plaque. If she'd only put things together a little sooner, maybe she could have saved Bronwin's life.

"You know what I don't understand?" she burst out. "Maud and Steve Rucker have been talking as if they're going to come into a whole lot of money. They've been shopping for expensive cars, making plans to fix up Maud's house—it doesn't make sense. For a while there I thought it might have some connection with the murder."

"You don't know about that? Yeah, I guess you wouldn't have heard. I only found out this morning at the office. Steve's made a big gold strike and he's cut his aunt in as a full partner. They're rich."

"What, gold in Casitas Creek?" Her voice rose in disbelief.

"No, no, that was just a ruse so people wouldn't take Steve seriously. Steve discovered a deposit of ore back in the hills, but he wanted to make sure his claim was official before he let the news out. He really was afraid of claim jumpers, you see. You can still get shot in this part of the country if the wrong person decides to move in on your land. Steve figured if he could get the town to laugh at him, he'd be free to come and go as he pleased. Now his claim has been formalized and he's sold the mine to a development company for a small fortune."

Carla shook her head in delighted amusement. "Good for him. Speaking of money, how's your job hunt going?"

"Not very well." Peter kicked a rock, sending it skittering down the street. "Jack Dwyer talked to his boss. It seems there's a serious shortage of the type of chips they need to build the machines that are in demand these days. The computer companies don't need any more salesmen to push their products. The problem is getting the computers built in the first place." He frowned, then waved a hand dismissively. "I've decided to look for work in some other field. I've already put a few feelers out."

"You know—" Carla's voice was thoughtful. She hesitated, then went on in a rush. "You've always liked your work with Cal-Equity Savings, until the company started going broke, that is. Now that Owen is moving the factory to town, your branch should start earning a profit. Why look for a new job when you've got a perfectly good one right here?"

They'd reached the stretch of sidewalk in front of their house. Peter stopped in his tracks, a bewildered look on his face. "But I thought you hated the Gold Country. You've been sulking ever since we left San Francisco. Now you're telling me you want to stay on in Placer Bar?"

She took his arm and led him up the driveway. "I've decided this town has possibilities."

Peter unlocked the door and they went in. Carla really looked at the living room for the first time in months. This wasn't a bad house, but it was a little seedy and neglected. The walls could use painting, the garden needed work and the kitchen would look brighter with a few plants on the windowsill. Maybe they could even get the landlord to pay for a new linoleum floor.

"I think I've taken on a new restoration project," she told him with a grin. "One that'll keep me busy for quite some time."

Printed in the United States
800400002B

9 781931 333221